CW00828875

Sin Bin 1

Iggy

Keith Miles

An Armada Original

Iggy was first published in Armada in 1988

Armada is an imprint of the Children's Division,
part of the Collins Publishing Group,
8 Grafton Street, London W1X 3LA

© 1988 Keith Miles

Printed in Great Britain by
William Collins Sons & Co. Ltd, Glasgow

Chapter One

Friday afternoon at Woodfield Comprehensive School meant a double period of chemistry. They hated it. Eighty minutes of organized boredom. Stuck on those hard plastic stools in the science lab. No chance of relief. No hope of talking to your friends. No prospect of a laugh even. Lambo saw to that. She was the kind of teacher who didn't let you get away with anything. Lambo was a sadist. All you could do in her lessons was to sit there and suffer.

Iggy put up with it for as long as he could then his gaze drifted to the window beside him. It was wet and cold outside and the scene was depressing. Rain fell steadily and a fierce wind was sweeping the playground. Winter had arrived with a vengeance.

Was there anything *worse* than double chem in December?

Roll on Christmas!

Iggy was a short, round, tubby boy of fourteen who always sat at the back of the class and tried to be inconspicuous. His big, blank face was a mass of freckles and his hair was close-cropped. He wore the regulation school uniform of grey trousers and a grey pullover with the school badge sewn on it. Yet he still managed to look spectacularly untidy. The large blue bag which lay at his feet bore the name and crest of Aston Villa Football Club. Iggy was a loyal fan.

He stared out through the glass and sighed.

Woodfield! What a joke!

Where was the wood? What happened to the field? No

sign of either. Nature had been killed off completely and replaced by a concrete jungle. The only timber that used to be visible was in the goal posts on the all-weather soccer pitch, but the posts had been stolen for firewood during a nocturnal raid and the new ones were made out of tubular steel. They had already been bent out of shape by swinging young vandals.

Woodfield! What a dump!

When Iggy looked beyond the school, he saw factories and warehouses and a multi-storey car park. In the distance were rows of ugly terraced houses, decrepit buildings that leaned against each other for support like drunken old men on their way home from the pub.

Iggy's attention came back to the pitch and he went off into a reverie. Wearing the famous claret and blue jersey of Aston Villa, he was playing at Wembley in a Cup Final. The teams were locked in a scoreless draw and time was running out. Then the ball was kicked high towards the Villa striker – Iggy.

Chesting it expertly down, he brought it under control before beating two defenders with the speed of his turn. He accelerated past a third man and reached the edge of the penalty area. As the goalkeeper came out to narrow the angle, Iggy chose his spot carefully then shot hard and low into the corner of the net.

It was a brilliant winning goal. Iggy held up his fist in triumph and punched the air.

'Higgins!'

He was too busy basking in the applause to hear Lambo.

'Higgins!'

The teacher's voice again failed to get through to him. Iggy was jumping for joy as the referee's whistle signalled the end of the match. His goal had won the Cup for Aston Villa.

'I'm talking to you, Ian Higgins!'

This time he had to take notice. Lambo yelled right into his ear then she took him by the shoulder and spun him around to face her. Iggy shuddered involuntarily. He'd rather be face to face with a grizzly bear.

Mrs Lambert was the fearsome Head of the Science Department. A tall, thin, imposing woman with well-groomed grey hair, she wore a white coat and always smelled faintly of disinfectant. You couldn't put an age on her. The pupils reckoned that she was anything between fifty and a hundred.

Lambo's eye was a laser beam that could burn the most unruly kids into submission. You didn't try it on with her. She was big trouble. Her voice was like the crack of a whip.

'What were you doing?' she demanded.

'Nuthin', miss.'

'Why weren't you *listening*?'

'Dunno, miss.'

'Why did you stare out through the window?'

'Dunno, miss.'

'Why did you ignore me when I spoke to you?'

'Dunno, miss.'

'Is there anything you *do* know, Higgins?' she mocked.

'Dunno, miss.'

'You're supposed to be in the middle of a chemistry lesson. Why do you think you come to the science laboratory?'

Iggy shrugged then heard himself saying the truth.

'To ger bored, miss.'

The whole class exploded into laughter. Lambo swung around and quelled them with another whiplash.

'Quiet!'

They fought to contain their mirth and watched eagerly.

The teacher turned both eyes on Iggy and gave him the full force of her laser power. But there was more than

7

naked venom in her stare. There was hurt surprise. Lambo had been caught off guard.

Ian Higgins of 4C was the last pupil from whom she would have expected any insolence. He was a shy, docile, self-conscious boy. Brighter than average but lazy. One of the could-do-betters.

But he was no troublemaker. Until today. She drew herself up to her full height to cow him.

'So you find my lessons boring, do you?'

'Dunno, miss.'

'I suppose you find *all* lessons rather tedious,' she continued sarcastically. 'I dare say you think that education is a load of rubbish.'

'Yeah, miss.'

The words slipped out before Iggy could stop them and their effect was immediate. Giggles echoed around the lab until the teacher cut them dead with a snarl. She pointed at Iggy.

'Come with me, Higgins!'

'Why, miss?'

'Do as I say, boy!'

Iggy recoiled from the sting of her tongue then he obeyed. He walked behind her to the front of the class then he stood before her desk. Lambo went up on to the dais to increase her eminence.

She made a grand, sweeping gesture with her hand.

'All right,' she invited. 'You take over.'

'Eh?'

'If my lessons are boring, let's see *you* teach.'

'Me, miss?' gulped Iggy.

'Yes – you, miss! Ian Higgins BSc. Dazzle us with your knowledge of chemistry. Hold us spellbound.'

There was a long pause. Iggy blushed.

'We're still waiting,' she teased. 'Fascinate us with your control of the subject. Demonstrate some complex experiments. Come on – *educate* us!'

A longer pause. A deeper blush. Sniggers. Lambo tormented him relentlessly.

Iggy was already the class joke. The fat kid with the funny face. The lone supporter of Aston Villa. Soccer-mad and yet hopeless at the game himself. Hopeless at everything the others could do. Like making friends and having fun.

He was used to ridicule. What Lambo was now inflicting on him was far worse. Utter humiliation. She was making an example of him in the most signal way. Iggy was mortified.

Then a strange thing happened. The pain began to ease. The more she went on, the less it hurt him. Instead of being wounded by her barbs, he became defiant. Anger stirred within him. Let her call him what she liked. He didn't care. Lambo was only a teacher.

He came through his ordeal with growing confidence.

'Briiing!' The school bell rescued him from further disgrace.

A groan of relief went up all round but it was quickly stifled by Lambo, who reminded them what their homework was and warned of dire consequences if they did not hand it in on Monday. When she dismissed them, they grabbed their bags and raced off. Free at last. The weekend beckoned.

Iggy started to walk back to his stool.

'Higgins!' snapped Lambo in a tone that stopped him in his tracks. 'Where do you think you're going?'

'I was goin' 'ome, miss.'

'Not yet.'

'Bur I gorra look after my sister, like.'

'You're staying here, young man.'

'Gail's waitin' for me, miss.'

'Let her wait.'

'Bur she'll ger upset.'

9

'You are not leaving this laboratory.'

'Doan worry,' said a voice. 'I'll pick up Gail.'

Samantha Jarrett was lingering in the doorway.

Unlike the rest of the class, she had not enjoyed Iggy's plight. Samantha – or Sam, as she was known – was sorry for him. A bright, chirpy, vivacious girl with dark, curly hair, she was a bit of a tomboy. She lived in the same block of flats as Iggy. Her younger brother, Kevin, went to the same school as Gail Higgins.

'I gorra fetch Kev,' she added. 'I'll ger Gail as well.'

Iggy was at once pleased and embarrassed by the offer. He was very fond of Sam but she somehow brought out his shyness. It was ironic. Friendly and open herself, she made him withdraw even more into his shell.

'Thanks,' he mumbled.

'Run along now, Samantha,' ordered Lambo.

'Yeah. OK. Bye, miss.'

'Goodbye.'

As Sam hurried out, Iggy gave a momentary smile. Someone cared about him. It helped to steel him against Lambo. The teacher crooked her finger to bring him back to a place directly in front of the desk again. His resentment smouldered but he did what she wanted. She fixed an eye on him to let him know that she was still very much in charge. Then she swung on her heel and went off into the room at the back of the lab.

While Iggy was kept waiting next door, she removed her white coat, folded it with care and put it into a plastic bag so that she could take it home to wash it. She then turned her attention to her briefcase, checking its contents to make sure that she had everything she needed.

Lambo now faced the mirror and adjusted her hair. The next task was to repair her make-up and she reached for her handbag. Before she could take anything out, however, she was distracted by a strong smell of smoke. Instinct

10

made her rush back into the lab. When she saw what was happening, her mouth dropped open in astonishment.

'Oh, my God!'

Iggy had lit the bunsen burner on the desk. After holding a sheet of paper in the flame, he had dropped it into the metal wastepaper bin. With calm unconcern, he was now feeding more paper in to keep the blaze going.

'What on earth are you *doing*!' she exclaimed.

Lambo acted with commendable speed and decision. Running to the far wall, she took down the fire extinguisher and released the safety lever before hurrying back to the small inferno. She aimed the nozzle of the appliance. High-pressure foam gushed out to subdue the fire in a matter of seconds. All that was left was the mess and the acrid smell. She switched off the bunsen burner and confronted Iggy. He didn't seem at all abashed. In fact, he was pleased with himself. Lambo was horrified.

David Parsons was less than delighted to see the Head of the Science Department bearing down on him. He was just leaving his office and was keen to get away from the school at the end of another trying week. The last thing he wanted was more hassle.

But Lambo was very determined.

'Could I have a word, headmaster?' she asked.

'Must you?' he sighed. 'Can't it wait until Monday?'

'I'm afraid not. It's a very serious matter.'

She glanced meaningfully at the fat boy beside her.

'Oh, very well, Mrs Lambert,' said the headmaster. 'Let's get it over with, shall we?'

He went into his office with a self-important swagger.

David Parsons was a man who hid his weakness behind an apparent show of strength. He was much given to huffing and puffing. His range of theatrical tricks was extensive but they had been used too often to have any effect.

He was short, squat, bow-legged and pot-bellied. Nature clearly intended him to have only one nickname and his optician clinched it by recommending a pair of black hornrimmed glasses. Woodfield's head was pure frog. Slimy but harmless. Froggie Parsons. He even croaked.

'Well?'

'This is Ian Higgins of 4C,' introduced Lambo.

'I know, I know,' said Froggie irritably. 'What is he supposed to have done, Mrs Lambert?'

'Set fire to the science laboratory.'

The headmaster couldn't have been more alarmed if someone had set fire to him. He slapped his desk with his hand, charged wildly about the room then stamped his foot like Rumpelstiltskin.

'This is *criminal*!'

Iggy said nothing. He was quite unruffled.

'What are the precise details?' urged Froggie. 'I want chapter and verse on this one, Mrs Lambert. It's an outrage!'

While Lambo told him the story, his face registered everything from terror to indignation. Froggie was on form. He could always be guaranteed to over-react.

'That's about it, headmaster,' she concluded.

'Appalling!'

'All we have to decide now is the punishment.'

'Quite so! Quite so!'

Froggie Parsons loved punishment. It distressed him that he was not able to dish out far more of it. The law kept getting in his way and the law was too soft. Froggie lived in a world of extremes. There were no half-measures.

He would cheerfully have made Iggy's crime a hanging offence. If it was up to him, truants would be transported.

Classroom bullies would be kept in chains. Thieves would be locked up in solitary confinement. He'd even bring back the birch for lateness.

Froggie assumed his favourite Napoleonic stance.

'This is one of the worst crimes that I have ever had to deal with in all my years as headmaster of Woodfield . . .'

It wasn't true but he made it sound as if it was.

'You, Higgins, have committed a heinous offence.'

Iggy was unworried. He glanced around the book-lined room without interest. Then he spotted the silver cup over the mantelpiece. It had been won by the school football team and he had longed to be part of the victorious eleven. As another reverie was set off, he was brought back to earth by Froggie's croak.

'This is a matter for the police.'

Iggy trembled. He was not ready for that.

'Oh, I don't think *that's* necessary,' said Lambo, coming to his rescue. 'I'm not playing down what Higgins did but it is his first real fall from grace. Most unlike him to misbehave in this way. It's not police business, headmaster.' She rammed home her point. 'Besides, we don't want any *more* bad publicity.'

'Er, no,' agreed Froggie. 'We certainly don't.'

Woodfield got into the headlines all too often. It caused a lot of problems and infuriated the education office. Froggie did not want any more unpleasant telephone calls from the authority. He was there to contain trouble and not to summon outside help.

'This is an internal affair,' insisted Lambo.

'You may be right.'

'A case of a short, sharp shock.'

Froggie took his cue. Turning to the boy, he glared at him through his spectacles then pointed a finger of doom at him.

'Higgins!'

'Sir?'

'On Monday morning at eight-thirty, you will present yourself to Mr Bowen at the Ainsley Annexe. He will be looking after your education for the next fortnight. I await his reports on your progress.' He stepped in closer. 'You do understand what goes on at the Annexe, don't you?'

Iggy nodded. He knew.

They were sending him to the Sin Bin.

Chapter Two

Clearview was a dilapidated block of council flats which gave its inhabitants a clear view of five similar blocks near the heart of the city. Concrete stairways and rows of iron railings ran up to the various levels. Graffiti artists had been busy on doors and walls and even windows. Messages of love and hate abounded.

The Higgins family lived on the top floor. Their flat was small, badly-designed and draughty. Rust lined the steel-framed windows. Ugly damp patches had spread across the ceilings but the council workmen – when they eventually came – could not cure them. The lavatory didn't flush properly and there was a regular problem with the hot water supply.

The furniture was old but serviceable and the carpets were secondhand. There were no pictures on the bare walls. Pride of place in the cramped living room went to the television. Newspapers and comics lay about. There was a general air of neglect.

Gail Higgins finished her bowl of Weetabix then looked anxiously at the clock on the wall of the kitchen. She got down from her chair and ran to the main bedroom to press an ear against the door. No sound came from within.

A small, plump nine year old girl, Gail had long ginger hair and the family freckles. Large wistful eyes shone out of her round face. She wore a plain dress and a thick cardigan.

After taking a deep breath, Gail knocked on the door. There was no answer. She let herself in to the darkened room.

'Mum!' she hissed. 'Mum!'

But her mother was still fast asleep, a slumbering mound beneath the blankets. The room was musty and untidy. Clothes and shoes were scattered everywhere. A heavy coat had been thrown on top of the bed to add extra warmth. An empty glass and a full ashtray stood on the bedside table.

The girl shook her mother gently by the shoulder.

'Mum – wake up.'

'Mm?'

'Please, Mum. Wake up.'

June Higgins opened one eye wide enough to take a bleary look at her daughter. She let out a deep moan and snuggled further under the bedclothes.

'It's time for school,' whispered Gail.

'Ian can take you,' murmured her mother.

'He won't.'

'He'll do as he's told.'

'I want *you* to take me, Mum.'

'I'm tired, Gail.'

At the third attempt, the lavatory flushed in the bathroom. Iggy soon appeared in the doorway and read the situation at once.

'You promised you'd take me,' reminded the girl.

'Tomorrow.'

'Oh, please, Mum.'

'Tomorrow!'

Gail gave up. She glanced at the open handbag on the floor.

'I need some money.'

'Borrow some,' grunted June.

'Bur I did thar last week. I still owe 'em.'

June Higgins rolled over to snap at her daughter.

'Look, doan bother me now, Gail! Carn you see I'm not

16

well? I had a very late night. I need a lie-in. Now, leave me alone, will you? Ger Ian to walk you to school.'

'I carn do thar,' said Iggy.

'You'll have to!' ordered his mother.

'Bur it'll make me late.'

'I told you,' said Gail.

'Gorra be there for 'alf past eight,' explained Iggy.

'You take me, Mum. *Please*.'

'Oh – sod off, the pair of you!'

June Higgins buried herself in the bedclothes once more. Gail turned tearful eyes towards her brother. Iggy glared at his mother with anger and disgust, then he threw a resigned glance at his sister. He nodded slowly.

Two minutes later, they were leaving the flat and stepping out into the ice-cold air. Iggy lifted his bicycle on to his shoulders and descended the eight flights of concrete steps. Gail trotted behind him, clutching her bag and trying not to shiver.

Another Monday morning had started

The Ainsley Annexe was on the corner of a road no more than fifty yards from Woodfield. It was a gracious Edwardian house which had been bequeathed to the education authority by a former Lord Mayor of the city. It was a valuable asset to an overcrowded school and Froggie Parsons knew exactly what to do with it.

The Annexe became a punishment block for wayward pupils. It was a dumping ground for kids who were too hot to handle. They were isolated from the main school and subjected to a stern regime. The idea was to make the place so unpleasant that nobody would ever wish to be sent back there.

Froggie Parsons was the only person who still called it the Ainsley Annexe. Everyone else knew it by another name. The Sin Bin.

It was full of sound and fury.

'Where the hell have *you* been?'

'Sorry, sir.'

'You were meant to be here at eight-thirty! Got that? Eight-bloody-thirty! That's when we open the cage for you horrible little animals. What time did I say?'

'Eight . . . thirty, sir.'

'Don't you forget it!'

Iggy had just arrived late at the Annexe.

He was greeted by the man who was in charge of the unit, Basher Bowen, a towering Welshman with a fist as big as a football and a voice that could be heard back in the valleys. Basher was the Dean of Discipline. After several years as Head of PE, he wanted a less strenuous job and he was a natural choice as Woodfield's hired gun.

Basher had a major advantage over all the kids. He was much bigger, stronger and wilder. A former Welsh ABA heavyweight champion, he was always willing to show off some of his punches. His jocular brand of violence was very effective.

He stared at Iggy from beneath beetle brows.

'I know you, don't I?' he said darkly.

'Ian 'iggins, sir. 4C.'

'That's it. Piggy Iggy. I've seen you waddling around the soccer pitch like a pregnant sow. You need to get some of that blubber off you, boyo. Understand?'

'Yeah, sir,' said Iggy nervously.

'Can't hear you.'

'Yeah, sir.'

'Speak up!'

'Yeah, sir!' called the boy.

'Don't you shout at me, you bladder of lard!'

Basher put his hands under Iggy's armpits and lifted him bodily off the ground so that the boy's feet dangled in midair.

18

The Dean of Discipline told him the rules.

'*I* run this place, Ian Higgins of 4C, and I run it my way. Got it? That means you don't so much as breathe round here without asking my permission first. You'll keep your nose to the grindstone and do everything I say. Otherwise, I'll eat you for breakfast and spit out the pips. OK?'

'Yeah . . . sir,' whispered Iggy in terror.

'As long as we see eye to eye.'

Basher put the boy down again and studied him for a moment. Bursting into laughter, he gave Iggy a playful punch.

'What's this I hear about you trying to set fire to Mrs Lambert, then?'

'No, sir. Thar wassen it, sir.'

'Don't you like old Lambo?'

'Yeah, sir.'

'Liar!'

'I didden set fire to 'er, sir.'

'That's not the way she tells it. According to Mrs Lambert, you tried to burn down the science lab with her in it. Who'd you think you are – Guy Fawkes?'

He rocked with mirth at his own joke then he became serious again. A huge palm was thrust beneath Iggy's nose.

'Right, boyo. Hand 'em over.'

'Wor, sir?'

'Matches.'

'Bur I gor none.'

'I'm not having fires here. If anyone goes up in flames, it'll be you. Now, give me the box.'

Iggy shook his head and gestured his innocence.

Basher searched him thoroughly with practised hands. He was disappointed when he found no matches on the boy.

'Don't you smoke?'

'No, sir.'

'Then you're the only kid here who doesn't. What about drink?'

'Drink, sir?'

'Beers, spirits, meths. You into booze of any kind?'

'No, sir.'

'Keep it that way. Are you any good in a scrap?'

'Nor really, sir.'

'Then you got problems. And not only from me.'

Basher led the way to a nearby door and pushed it open with a flourish. Iggy followed him into what had once been the spacious living room of the house. It was now the main classroom and had been fitted out with desks. A dozen boys stood up from their seats as Basher surged in.

He made sure that they were all standing politely to attention then he waved them down again. With an arm around Iggy, he faced the class.

'You all know who this is. Ian Higgins of 4C.'

The boys were amazed. Iggy was not Sin Bin material.

'He's been having us on,' continued Basher. 'We thought he was just a fat slob who was too fond of his bangers and mash. But no! Underneath this law-abiding exterior, we got something a lot more dangerous. A pyromaniac. That means he likes starting fires. Don't you, boyo?'

'No, sir.'

'Of course you do!'

'Yeah, sir.'

'Make up your mind!'

'Yeah, sir . . . no, sir . . .'

'Three bags full, sir!'

The others smirked at Iggy's expense. He risked a quick look around the room and quailed. The twelve faces that were leering at him belonged to the worst thugs, bullies and petty criminals in the school. Iggy was not among friends.

Basher pushed him down into an empty desk.

'Sit there and stay there.'

'Yeah, sir.'

He handed Iggy a book and a pad of loose leaf paper. The rest of the class watched with amusement. Basher glowered at them.

'Haven't you lot got any work to do?'

Twelve heads bent over the desks. A dozen cheap biros were soon in action. The working day had begun. Basher turned back to Iggy and drew his attention to the marker in the book.

'Mrs Lambert sent that. She's marked the chapter for you. Something about acids. That's what you should have been learning on Friday afternoon instead of playing with matches. Learn it now. Copy it out in your best hand-writing. Got it?'

'Yeah, sir.'

'When you finish, put your hand up.'

'Yeah, sir.'

'But don't speak.'

'No, sir.'

'Don't speak!' bellowed the Welshman from close range then he grinned broadly. 'We got a rule of silence here. Just like in a monastery. Go on, Brother Iggy. Get weaving.'

Iggy took out his pen and set about his chore. He didn't dare to look up. The place was much smaller, cleaner and cosier than the classrooms in the main school but its atmosphere was hostile and repressive. Iggy was the thir-teenth pupil there. It was a bad omen.

Basher pulled a copy of the *Daily Mirror* from his pocket and started to read it. An hour or more passed. On the stroke of ten, the teacher dispatched one of the boys to go and make him a cup of tea. It arrived with two biscuits in the saucer. The boy resumed his seat.

Another hour passed. The tea boy went through the same routine. It was evident that the pupils got no mid-morning break at the Annexe. They simply slaved on.

Iggy finished copying out the chapter and put his pen down. He sat upright and raised his hand but Basher took no notice. The boy had to keep his arm aloft for several minutes before the teacher glanced up from his crossword.

'What d'you want, boyo?'

'Please, sir – I done it.'

'Pass it here.'

Iggy handed him the seven pages of closely-written text. Basher treated them to a look of disdain before screwing them up and throwing them into the wastepaper basket.

'*Best* handwriting,' he insisted.

'Yeah, sir.'

'Start again.'

The prospect made Iggy's heart sink but he had no choice. Turning back to the beginning of the chapter, he gritted his teeth and did as he was told.

At one o'clock, they were allowed a half-hour break for lunch. They were sent out into the walled garden at the rear of the house. It was little more than a courtyard and all they could do was to lounge and chat. The ten pupils from the other class at the Annexe joined them. Four were girls. Iggy wondered what they had done to get themselves sent to the Sin Bin.

They were still under surveillance. The staff room was on the first floor. Basher Bowen sat in the window with a cheese roll in his hand. There was no freedom at the Annexe. Someone was always watching. It was very unsettling.

Iggy went off into a corner to be on his own but he was not left there for long. Three boys sidled over to him and stood in a half-circle around him. He recognized them at

22

once. Mark Stavros, Pug Anderson and Elroy Cooper. The hard lads of 5B.

They were a year older and smarter than Iggy and he was intimidated by them. Mark was the leader of the gang, a tall, dark, athletic youth with flashy good looks that made the girls flock after him. Pug was the muscle man, a thickset boy with a severe acne problem. Elroy, a grinning West Indian, was the joker in the pack. Mark appraised the new boy.

'Gor any grub?' he asked.

'Yeah,' admitted Iggy.

'Give it 'ere,' said the other.

'You woan need it,' added Elroy. 'You're on a diet, man.'

'Yeah,' agreed Pug. 'We're doin' you a favour, like.'

Before he could stop them, they grabbed him and ransacked his pockets for the fish paste sandwiches he had made for himself before leaving the flat. Mark unwrapped the paper and shared out the booty. Munching happily, the three of them went off into the building. Two of the girls followed.

Iggy looked up to the staff room for help but the Dean of Discipline was gazing steadily out over the city. The boy got the message. Basher only saw what he wanted to see. Iggy was on his own. There was no court of appeal.

Others now closed in on him to tease and interrogate and bully. Iggy turned puce when one of the girls threatened to kiss him. He kept wishing the bell would go to end the lunch break.

A Pakistani youth ran out of the building.

'Hey – Iggy!'

'Yeah?'

'Basher wants you. Quick!'

Iggy glanced upwards. No teacher at the window.

'Where is 'e?'

23

'In the storeroom. I'll show you.'

The Pakistani loped off and Iggy followed. He knew that Basher would not want to be kept waiting. When they got back into the house, the guide pointed to a door at the end of the passageway. It was slightly ajar.

'In there. Knock and go in.'

Iggy obeyed and walked straight into the trap.

Mark, Pug and Elroy were ready for him. The two girls were there to watch the fun. As soon as he went through the doorway, Iggy was tripped up and went sprawling on to the bare floor. A bag of flour was tipped over him and a bucket of water came next. Laughter mocked him.

The three attackers left with the girls and shut the door behind them. Chalked on the back of it was a message. When Iggy wiped away the sticky mess from his eyes, he was able to read what it said.

WELCOME TO THE SIN BIN!

He'd never felt so alone in all his life.

Chapter Three

Cameron Road Junior School was almost a century old and it was showing its age. The building was grimy and its brickwork was in urgent need of repointing. Ancient green paint was flaking off the doors and windows. A number of slates on the pitched roof were either cracked or missing. The cowl had long since disappeared from the chimney. On a cold December afternoon, the place looked very forlorn.

School ended at three-thirty but Gail Higgins did not go straight home. She preferred to wait until her brother was able to pick her up. Cameron Road was a main thorough-fare into the city and there were many other busy roads to negotiate on the way back to Clearview. Gail was not the only pupil who waited to be taken home by an elder brother or sister. Nine or ten children were in the same position and a member of staff stayed behind to keep an eye on them until they were collected.

As Gail lounged against a wall in the playground, she watched Kevin Jarrett running about with a couple of friends. Kevin was a short, stocky boy with unlimited energy. There was a strong resemblance between him and his sister but they were very different in other ways. While Samantha Jarrett was a generous and responsible girl, her brother was selfish and headstrong. He had all the makings of a tearaway.

Gail was in the same class as Kevin but she usually kept out of his way. He was far too rough for her. The only time he bothered with girls was to tease them or pull their hair.

'Kev!'

Sam had a powerful pair of lungs. Her voice rose above the drone of the traffic and echoed around the playground.

'Come on, Kev!'

'OK!' he yelled back.

'*Now*!'

'Keep your 'air on!'

Reluctantly breaking away from his game, he picked up his bag and trotted off. His sister did not like to be kept hanging about. She would only nag him if he dawdled. And Sam was almost as good a nagger as their mother.

Gail saw her own brother cycling towards the school and she strolled across towards him. All four of them met up at the main gate. Iggy was shamefaced. Still jangled by his first day in the Annexe, he did not wish to speak to anyone, especially to Sam. All he wanted to do was to go home and lock himself in his own room.

But Sam was in an inquisitive mood.

'How was it?' she asked.

'Wor?' muttered Iggy.

'The Sin Bin.'

'Oh . . . that.'

'Is it as bad as they say it is?'

'Sort of.'

'Wor did they do to you?'

'Nuthin' much.'

'Less go,' said Kevin bluntly.

'Shurrup!' warned his sister.

'Bur I'll miss the telly,' he complained.

'This is important,' she said, turning back to Iggy with intense curiosity. 'Go on. Tell us wor 'appened, like.'

But he could never do that. He could never tell anyone about the horrors of his initiation in the storeroom at the Annexe. The memory of it all made his brain swim. Iggy

26

could still feel the flour in his hair and the water seeping through his clothes. The Sin Bin had been slow torture.

'Well?' pressed Sam.

'Basher made us work all the time,' grunted Iggy.

'Thass all?'

'Thass all.'

Admiration now came into her eyes. She smiled proudly at Iggy as if seeing him properly for the first time. Her attitude towards him subtly changed.

'Never thort you 'ad it in you.'

'Wor?'

'Takin' on Lambo like thar.'

'Oh . . . yeah.'

'Settin' fire to them papers in the lab,' she said. 'Thar took a lot of courage. You're really brave.'

'Am I?'

It had never occurred to him before. Iggy had lit the bunsen burner on impulse. He still did not understand why. It certainly hadn't been a case of outstanding bravery. He just did it.

'The rest of the class carn believe it,' continued Sam.

'Why nor?'

'They never thort you'd stand up to 'er like you did.'

'Wor about my telly?' whined Kevin, only to get a clout for his interruption. 'Aouw!'

'Serves you right,' said his sister before giving Iggy another warm smile. 'Yeah, you really surprised 'em.'

'Did I?'

'Course. Takes a lor to ger sent to the Sin Bin. You're a kind of 'ero now. Tara, Ian.'

She waved a hand and walked away with her brother.

Iggy blinked in sheer astonishment. Sam Jarrett had actually praised him. The rest of the class looked up to him. It changed everything. Instead of skulking off home after the miseries of his day at the Annexe, he could hold

27

up his head in pride. The Sin Bin conferred status on him. He was special. As he recalled Sam's last two words, 'Tara, Ian,' he beamed. It was the first time for years she'd used his real name.

Gail Higgins was bemused by it all. Her face was one big frown of bewilderment. Something was going on.

'Wass this Sin Bin?' she wondered.

'Never mind.'

'You tell Mum abour it?'

'No,' he said firmly. 'And you woan tell 'er either.'

'You gor into trouble or somethin'?'

'Less go 'ome.'

As they headed in the direction of Clearview, Iggy made sure that Sam did not get too far in front of him. He liked the way her hair bobbed up and down as she strode along. He loved the way her shoes clacked on the pavement.

The conversation with her redeemed his whole day. He had seen himself as a victim but his classmates thought differently. Not only did he tell Lambo that her lessons were boring, he started a fire in her wastepaper bin. That took real daring.

Iggy was a hero. It made him feel good.

Basher Bowen poured himself a cup of steaming black coffee and spooned in plenty of sugar. He stirred the mixture vigorously before tasting. Then he went to flop down in a battered armchair opposite Don Sheen, one of his colleagues.

'I'll see him first thing tomorrow,' said Don.

'No point,' advised Basher.

'But I like a chat with every kid we get.'

'This one won't be there long enough.'

'We have him for a fortnight, surely?'

'Iggy won't last the week.'

It was early evening and they were in the staff room at

the main school. Woodfield never closed. As well as being a big inner city comprehensive, it was a community college that offered a wide range of classes. You could learn anything from cake decorating to car maintenance. That evening alone there were courses on maths, home economics, typewriting, computer literacy, basic Spanish, photography, flower arranging and the history of railways.

Like many others on the staff, Basher and Don supplemented their income by taking evening classes. The Welshman would be in charge of badminton coaching in the sports hall while the other would be teaching introductory psychology.

Don Sheen was really committed to his job. A lively and intelligent young man, he had a degree in social sciences and a burning desire to put it to use in his home town. Now in his late twenties, Don still had his distinctive Midlands accent.

'I'll have a crack at Higgins tomorrow,' he decided.

'Waste of time, mun.'

'The kid needs help.'

'He needs a kick up his fat arse, that's all.'

'I want to understand why he started the fire.'

'Would *you* fancy double chem with Lambo?' asked Basher. 'Must be bloody murder. That woman bores the drawers off me when she asks me the time of day. Just imagine eighty minutes of it. No wonder Iggy reached for a box of matches.'

'There's more to it than that, Bryn.'

'Not in my book.'

The Sin Bin was not just a way of punishing the pupils. It could also be used as a weapon against the staff. Awkward or outspoken teachers could find themselves timetabled to do a stint at the Annexe. It was Froggie's means of revenge.

Don Sheen was the exception to the rule. While everyone

else tried to steer clear of the place, he volunteered to work there. Don and Basher were now the two permanent figures at the Sin Bin. Their methods differed.

'We have to get to the root cause,' argued Don.

'The root cause is simple. Kids hate school.'

'It goes deeper than that.'

'Well, I'm not digging for it.'

'The Sin Bin ought to rehabilitate.'

'Rubbish!'

'OK. What do *you* think it should do?'

'Put the fear of death into the little blighters.'

'That doesn't work, Bryn.'

'Yes, it does. Up to a point.'

'Behaviour problems need to be probed.'

'They need to be sat on – hard!'

Although the two men disagreed about the way to run the Annexe, they remained close friends. Their arguments were always good-humoured. Don Sheen was a young idealist while Basher Bowen was a cynical realist. They made an interesting team.

Don would not be shifted from his decision.

'I'll have a session with Higgins in the morning.'

'You won't get the chance, boyo.'

'Why not?'

'Because he won't be there,' said Basher. 'Stavros and his mates put Iggy through the hoops. They scared the living daylights out of him. My guess is that he won't come anywhere near the Sin Bin tomorrow.'

June Higgins got home as usual around six o'clock. She worked in the afternoons at the checkout in Sainsbury's and she always came back tired and irritable. Today it was different. She brought a Mars bar for Iggy and Gail. She even gave them a token kiss.

'Oo! Thanks, Mum!' said the girl, unwrapping the chocolate.

'Save it till you've had your tea,' urged her mother.

'This *is* my tea.'

'Have it as your pudding.'

But Gail could not wait. While June prepared a meal of fish fingers and baked beans, her daughter chewed her way happily through the Mars bar. By the time she had swallowed the last of it, there was a circle of chocolate around her mouth.

'Look at the state you're in!' scolded June.

'Wass wrong, Mum?'

'You're supposed to eat the thing, not use it as a lipstick. Go to the bathroom and clean yourself up, girl.'

Gail went off and the tap was soon heard running.

Iggy watched it all in silence. He was pleased that his mother was in a better mood but he was still wary. She could be volatile. It didn't take much to upset her these days.

'How was school, Ian?' she asked.

'OK.'

'Wor did you do?'

'Nor much.'

'Any homework?'

'I done it already,' he lied.

June divided up the fish fingers and put them on to the three separate plates. She added the beans then set the meal on the table. Her tone was casual.

'I'll be goin' out tonight,' she said.

'Where to?'

'For a drink. With the girls from work.'

'Bur you did thar last night,' he reminded her. 'And Saturday.'

'I've gorra have some fun out of life,' she retorted with a slight edge. 'You carn expect me to stay in all the time.'

31

'Yeah. I know.'

They took their seats in the little kitchen and Gail came in to join them. She reached for the tomato sauce and covered her fish fingers in it. Iggy could not bear to look as his sister shovelled the first load into her mouth. He attacked his beans.

June laughed as she recalled an incident at work.

'They cort another shoplifter today.'

'Who was it?' said Gail with immediate interest.

'Some woman in this long coat, like. With these great big pockets sewn into it. Mr Matthews – our store detective – thort there was somethin' funny about her from the way she walked.'

'Wor did 'e do, Mum?' asked Gail.

'Followed her out. All she paid for at the checkout was a packet of sweets and a jar of pickled onions. Then Mr Matthews taps her on the shoulder, like. "Would you like to come to the manager's office?" he says. "No," she says, "I damn well wouldn't." And she runs off like she's in the Olympics.'

'Did 'e catch 'er?' said the girl.

'In the precinct,' explained June. 'If she hadn't pinched so much, she might've gor away. Bur it slowed her down, see? When they searched her pockets, they found biscuits, washin' powder, jellies, filter coffee, cheese, butter, bacon, three tins of cat food and a bottle of aspirin. She was a branch of Sainsbury's in herself!'

Gail shared her mother's laughter but Iggy was not drawn in. His mind was on something else. When he put his question, it wiped the smile straight off their faces.

'When's Dad comin' 'ome?'

June glared at him for even raising the subject.

'Where is 'e?' persisted the boy.

'Workin' away,' she replied.

'You always say thar.'

32

'It's the truth.'

'Why duzzen 'e write? Or send a postcard?'

'Ask him.'

'Bur I doan know where 'e is.'

'Neither do I.'

June dismissed the topic by getting up from the table to put the kettle on. Her good mood had evaporated now. She banged about for several minutes and whisked their plates from the table as soon as they had been cleared. After making herself a cup of tea, she took it into the bathroom and locked the door. They could hear a bath being drawn.

Gail turned angrily on her brother.

'Wor did you ask thar for?' she accused.

'I wanna know where Dad is.'

'Mum duzzen.'

'Well, I do!'

Iggy went into his tiny bedroom and closed the door. He lay down to brood. It was over a month since his father had gone and he still hadn't had a full explanation from his mother. Iggy looked at the team photographs of Aston Villa that were plastered all over his walls. His father was from Birmingham and he had taken his son back from time to time to watch his old team play. They had been magical afternoons and Iggy treasured them.

But they seemed to have gone for ever now.

An hour later, June had put on another dress, done her make-up and was ready to leave. Gail was watching *Coronation Street* and Iggy was still in his room. His mother thumped on his door.

'Ian!'

'Yeah?'

'Gail's gorra be in bed by nine.'

'Aw, Mum!' protested the girl.

'And you're not to stay up after ten. OK, Ian?'

'OK,' he muttered.

'If I'm nor up in the mornin', doan wake me.'

June gave her daughter another token kiss and swept out. Iggy felt very uneasy. He might be a hero to his class but he was anything but that at home. His father had been his real friend and Aston Villa had become a lifeline. Iggy had lost both. Yet he did not really know why.

When nine o'clock came around, there were further protests from Gail and she had to be bribed with half of her brother's Mars bar. As soon as she was in bed, Iggy himself retired. He lay beneath the sheets with his hands clasped behind his head.

Various people crowded into his mind. He thought about Basher Bowen at the Annexe. About Mark Stavros and his two mates. About Lambo. About Sam Jarrett and her brother. About his own mother and sister. Finally – and inevitably – he thought about his father. If only *he* would come back everything would be all right.

Iggy soon dozed off in the darkness.

His dream was only an extension of his reverie. He heard the sound of a key in the front door then his father came in to announce a surprise. He had two tickets for a cup tie between Aston Villa and Birmingham City. It was a local derby that was bound to produce plenty of goals and action. Iggy was thrilled.

Vance Higgins had come home at last.

'Where you been?' asked the boy.

'I'll tell you some time.'

'You back for good now?'

'Oh yeah, son. For good!'

The pledge brought Iggy awake.

In a flash, he moved from dream to reality. His father *was* there. He could hear the familiar deep voice in the living room. His mother's laughter showed how pleased she was to have her husband at her side once more. There was a clink of glasses. They were obviously celebrating his return.

Iggy clambered out of bed and groped for the door handle. Blinking against the sudden light, he padded along the passage to the living room and burst in.

'Welcome home, Dad!' he said.

The two figures on the sofa regarded him in surprise. His mother was stunned and the man beside her was annoyed. He was not Vance Higgins at all. He was much younger and far less friendly.

'Wor d'you wann, kid?' he challenged.

'Go back to bed at once!' snapped June.

Iggy retreated as fast as he could. He was not wanted.

Chapter Four

Mark Stavros sauntered along the road towards Woodfield with his hands thrust deep into the pockets of his jacket. Pug Anderson was at his side, chewing gum and blowing an occasional bubble with it. Elroy Cooper was a few paces behind them, dancing to the beat of the song he was humming.

The three friends were trying to decide on something.

'Less throw 'im in the canal,' suggested Pug.

'No,' said Mark.

'Why nor?'

'Thass goin' too far.'

'Pinch 'is bike,' volunteered Elroy.

'Wor use is thar to us?'

'Yeah,' agreed Pug. 'Crappy old thing.'

Mark pondered. 'There's gorra be somethin'.'

Elroy clapped his hands and whooped with delight.

'Stick a dead mouse down his neck!'

'Or a live rat,' said Pug with a cackle.

'Why nor a dog or a cat?' mocked their leader. 'Why nor an 'erd of sheep. Talk sense, will you? Where do we ger animals from? Anyway, thar kind of stuff's too corny. Iggy deserves berra. So use your brains.'

'Wor brains?' asked Elroy.

'Good question!' retorted Mark.

'Why doan we nick his bag?' offered Pug.

'Cos it says Aston-flippin'-Villa all over it!'

'Oh, yeah. Sorry, Mark.'

'Honess, Pug. You ger stupider every day.'

'Practice makes perfect!' teased Elroy.

Pug kicked at a discarded cigarette packet and sent it spinning into the gutter. He knew that his two friends were much more intelligent than he was but he didn't like to be reminded of the fact. There was something else which set them apart from him and it hurt even more.

'Hey, Mark!'

'Are you goin' tonight?'

'Wor about you, Elroy?'

'See you there, Mark!'

'We'll be waitin'!'

The three girls were just going in through the main gate. They called excitedly to Mark and Elroy but they did not even notice Pug. He just did not have the touch where girls were concerned. If they went to the disco that night, it would be the same old story. Mark and Elroy would dance all the time and Pug would be stuck on the sidelines with a drink in his hand.

They came to a halt and watched the pupils streaming into the school. Mark waved to a few more girls. Elroy hummed another pop song. Pug tried to assert himself by coming up with what he thought was a bright idea.

'I gorrit!'

'You could've fooled me,' joked Elroy.

'Why doan we nick all his clothes?'

'Who?'

'Iggy 'iggins. Then 'e'd 'ave to run round starkers.'

'Thass a mad idea,' said Mark scornfully. 'Who wants to look at 'im with 'is clothes off? Be like a baby elephant.'

'Leave the thinkin' to us, Pug,' advised Elroy.

'Bur you gor no plan either.'

'We will 'ave, man.'

'Only a question of time,' said Mark confidently.

At that moment, a large new estate car came swishing down the road with its indicator flashing. Sounding its horn to clear the pupils out of the way, it turned in through

37

the main entrance and headed for the staff car park. They had all seen the figure who was crouched at the wheel. It was Lambo.

Mark and Elroy exchanged a knowing smile. They had settled on an idea at last.

'Wor is it?' asked Pug. 'Wor is it?'

'You'll see,' promised Mark.

'Yeah,' said Elroy with a grin. 'So will Lambo.'

Basher Bowen's prediction was wrong. Iggy turned up on time that morning and went silently to his desk. The boy had not been frightened away. He was back for more.

As soon as registration was over, Iggy was sent upstairs to see Don Sheen. The teacher took him into a small bedroom that was now used as an office. It contained a desk, a filing cabinet and a couple of chairs. On the wall was a calendar with a view of the Lake District. Beside the telephone was a cassette recorder.

'Take a pew,' invited Don.

'Yeah, sir.'

'And relax. Nobody's going to hurt you.'

Iggy sat in front of the desk. Don perched on the edge of it and smiled down at the boy in an attempt to put him at his ease. It had the opposite effect. Sullen and preoccupied when he came in, Iggy was now watchful and defensive.

Basher was bad enough but at least you knew where you were with him. Don Sheen was not like that. He was keen on psychology. He wanted to talk to you and get inside your mind. Iggy was scared. Nervous tension made him begin to sweat.

'What do you think of the Sin Bin?' asked Don.

The boy's face was impassive. He made no reply.

'Would you rather be back at the main school?'

There was a pause then Iggy nodded.

'Why?'

All he got by way of an answer was a slight shrug.

Don moved to the chair behind the desk and leaned back in it. He was a slovenly man in old denims, a creased black shirt and a leather jacket that curled up at the edges. His lank hair was thick and long. His face was kind.

Iggy had never been taught by him but he knew all the stories. Don's nickname was Mister Softee because he would usually just talk to the kids instead of punishing them. But Iggy found the talk itself a punishment. The teacher was trying to drag something out of him that he did not want to yield up. Mister Softee worried him. Iggy would settle for Basher any day.

'You're angry, aren't you, Ian?' resumed Don.

'No, sir.'

'You are. Question is – who are you angry *with*?'

'Nobody, sir.'

'Is it Mr Parsons?'

'No, sir.'

'Are you angry with Froggie for sending you here?'

'No, sir.'

'Well, you can't be *pleased* about it.'

'No, sir.'

'What about Basher? You angry with him?'

'No, sir.'

'Or me?'

Iggy shook his head. He was now very uncomfortable.

'Is it Mark Stavros and his pals, then?' suggested Don. 'I know they gave you a rough ride yesterday. They do it to everyone who comes here. Are you angry with them?'

'No, sir.'

'Well, you ought to be. Ganging up on you like that.'

Iggy shrugged again and shifted in his chair. It was hard going with Mister Softee. He kept trying to get in under your guard. He wanted to break you wide open.

Don leaned forward across the desk and nodded.

'I know who it is. Lambo. You're angry with her.'

'No, sir!' denied the boy vehemently.

'You'd have to be, lad,' argued the teacher. 'Only anger could make you stand up to her the way you did. Lambo is as tough as old boots. Basher used to be a boxer, but even *he* wouldn't fancy going three rounds with Lambo.' He sat back in his chair again. 'Yes, that's it. You're angry with Lambo.'

'Bur I'm nor, sir!'

'Then there's only one person left, Ian.'

'Eh?'

'You're angry with yourself.'

There was enough truth in the remark to jolt Iggy.

He was not enjoying the conversation. Given the choice, he would rather be copying out chapters from his chemistry book. That was a chore but it did not rattle him in the way that all these questions did. He got another jolt when the teacher reached forward to switch on the cassette recorder. Iggy stared at it as if it were some instrument of torture.

Seeing the boy's alarm, Don switched the machine off then put it away in a drawer. He tried a second smile but it broke no more ice than the first. Iggy had clammed up.

'What's your favourite subject?' asked the teacher.

No reply. The pupil was feeling vulnerable.

'I see you're a Villa fan.'

Even that did not get through. Don was surprised. He moved on to a different tack. Standing up behind the desk, he made a dismissive gesture with both hands.

'That's about it, then. You can go now.'

Iggy got to his feet at once and shuffled to the door.

'One last thing, Ian . . .' said Don casually.

'Yeah, sir?'

'What does your father do?'

'My dad?'

'Does he have a regular job?'

'Oh, yeah,' replied Iggy with a show of spirit. "e's a driver. Gor this big van. Dad delivers furniture and thar.'

'What about your mother?'

'Mum?'

'Does she work as well?'

'Yeah. Afternoons in Sainsbury's, like.'

'Two wage earners in one family,' noted Don. 'That's good. And not all that common at Woodfield. A lot of our fathers are unemployed. Especially among the ethnic minorities. It's often the mothers who bring in the only wage. That can put strains on a marriage.' He opened the door and led Iggy out. 'Er . . . your parents still live together, don't they?'

'Course!' said the boy with a hint of panic.

But they both knew it was a lie.

The interview was over. Don Sheen had made progress.

Cameron Road Junior School exploded into noise during the mid-morning break. Kids raced around the playground, laughing, shouting, screaming or crying. Games were played, arguments were started, old scores were settled. The teacher on duty was kept as busy as ever.

Gail Higgins was talking to her best friend in a corner of the yard. The girls found the horseplay too boisterous for them. They preferred to chat about what they would like for Christmas. It was Mandy Swales, the best friend, who gave the warning.

'Look out, Gail!'

'Why?'

'That Kevin Jarrett's comin' over.'

'We doan wanna speak to 'im,' said Gail, turning away.

'Well, 'e's gonna speak to one of us.'

Nothing was going to stop Kevin. He had the cheerful

grin of someone who has special news to impart. After winking at Mandy, he prodded Gail on the shoulder.

'Lissen,' he said. 'I wanna word with you.'

'Go away!' she snapped, keeping her back to him.

'Yeah,' added her friend. 'Leave 'er alone.'

'You stay out of this, Mandy Swales,' he warned.

'Aw, shurrup!' she retaliated.

'I'll bash you in a minute!'

'Then I'll tell Miss Norton on you.'

'Juss like you!' he sneered. 'Bandy Mandy! Telltale tit!'

Gail swung round to face him. Her arms were folded.

'Stop callin' 'er names, Kevin Jarrett.'

'She was pokin' 'er big nose in.'

'Mandy is my best friend.'

'So shove off!' ordered the other girl.

The grin reappeared on Kevin's face. He sniggered.

'Talkin' of best friends . . .'

'Wor you on about?' asked Gail.

'Your mum,' he teased. 'She's gorra best friend.'

'Shut your gob!' howled Mandy.

'My dad saw 'em boozin' together down the pub,' continued Kevin. 'Says 'e didden know Mrs 'iggins 'ad a boyfriend.'

'Snor true!' cried Gail.

'Arsk your mum, then!'

'Doan lissen to 'im, Gail,' advised Mandy.

'Wass the boyfriend's name?' jeered Kevin.

'Make 'im shurrup!' pleaded Gail, putting her hands over her ears. 'Make 'im go away.'

Mandy pushed the boy hard and he ran away.

But the damage had already been done. Gail's lower lip quivered then the tears came in a flood. Mandy put a consoling arm around her and eased her across some stone steps where they sat down. Dabbing at her eyes with a handkerchief, Gail tried to pretend that it was a lie. Kevin was making it up. Mandy gave her all the comfort she could and urged her to ignore what she was told. Kevin only said it out of spite.

When Gail finally calmed down, it was her best friend's turn to look for reassurance. Mandy studied her legs.

'Gail . . .'

'Wor?'

'I'm nor *really* bandy, am I?'

Iggy was shattered. The session with Don Sheen had been followed by hours of gruelling work with Basher Bowen. By the time the lunch break arrived, Iggy was exhausted. Yet now he would have to run the gauntlet again. He gathered up the last of his strength to withstand the taunts and the bullying.

But they did not come. Instead of pushing him around and taking his sandwiches, Mark, Pug and Elroy wanted to befriend him. They were actually on his side.

'Lambo is to blame,' announced Mark.

'Yeah,' said Elroy. 'She dropped you in it.'

'You oughta ger your own back,' grunted Pug.

'Like the idea?' asked Mark.

'Well . . .' Iggy was uncertain.

'You doan belong in 'ere,' argued Elroy. 'It was Lambo who gor you dumped on us.'

'Iss about time someone 'it back at 'er,' offered Pug.

'So we've chosen you, mate,' explained Mark confidentially. 'Wass more, we're gonna 'elp you. Right, lads?'

'Right,' confirmed Pug.

'With you all the way, man!' said Elroy.

Iggy was both flattered and mystified. His face puckered.

'Wor do I 'ave to do?'

Mark smiled lazily. 'Know thar new car of Lambo's?'

'Yeah.'

'Thass your target, Ig.'

43

'Go gerrit!' urged Pug.

'Search and destroy!' said Elroy, slapping him on the back for encouragement. 'You can do it.'

'Maybe,' replied Iggy. 'Bur . . .'ow?'

'Stick a bomb under it and blow it sky 'igh!' suggested Pug.

Iggy's eyes widened until they almost popped out.

'Doan lissen to Pug,' said Mark easily. 'There's no need for bombs or anythin' like thar. Juss attack the car in some way. Leave your mark on it. Tell 'im, Elroy.'

'I done dozens,' boasted the West Indian. 'Me and my brother did seven in a pub car park one night. We broke off aerials, like. We kicked in 'eadlights. We sprayed the windscreens. Yeah, we even took off a roof rack. Still gorrit back 'ome.'

'Wor am I supposed to do to Lambo's car?' asked Iggy.

'Take your pick,' invited Elroy.

'Yeah,' said Pug. 'Pour a bag of sugar in 'er petrol tank, if you like. Or nick 'er sparkin' plugs.'

'Make up your mind when you do the job,' advised Mark.

'When's thar?' wondered Iggy.

'After school.'

'*Today*!'

'Why nor?'

'Bur I carn!' protested Iggy.

'Iss gorra be today,' reasoned Mark. 'Staff meeting as soon as school ends. Basher told us.'

'Lambo'll be stuck in that,' Elroy pointed out. 'That new car of 'ers will be waitin' for you. You juss nip in the car park and – bingo!'

'I will,' conceded Iggy, 'only nor today.'

'Why?' demanded Pug.

'I gorra pick up my sister from Cameron Road.'

'This woan take long,' said Mark. 'Your sister can 'ang on for another five minutes, carn she?'

'She'll 'ave to,' insisted Pug.

'This is your big chance, Ig,' instructed Elroy. 'You can ger your revenge on Lambo while 'er back is turned. Might be ages before there's another staff meeting.'

Iggy bit his lip. He was very apprehensive.

'We're countin' on you,' said Mark.

'Doan chicken out now,' warned Pug.

'We keep watch,' said Elroy. 'You do the job.'

'Only take two minutes,' continued Mark. 'Then you can ger on your bike and shoot off to Cameron Road. S'all set up.'

Iggy was still hesitating. The three friends traded a glance then applied the last bit of pressure. They moved in close so that they could whisper into his ear.

'You gonna ler Lambo ger away with it?' asked Elroy.

'Show the old bitch!' grunted Pug.

'She bunged you in 'ere!' reminded Elroy.

'Teach 'er a lesson!' hissed Pug.

Mark Stavros produced the most convincing argument.

'Do this – and you'll be one of us, like.'

Iggy was thrilled. He felt a surge of importance.

'Wor d'you say?' pressed Mark. 'Will you do it?'

'Yeah!'

They congratulated him warmly and made him feel accepted. Iggy actually began to look forward to his attack on Lambo's car.

So did the others.

But, then, they knew what was really going to happen.

Chapter Five

Samantha Jarrett ran along the pavement in Cameron Road at a steady speed. She was a natural athlete who knew how to pace herself. When she reached the school, she was not even out of breath. Leaning on the gate, she scanned the playground for her brother. As usual, Kevin was tearing about with some other boys. Sam was going to call him when she noticed someone else.

It was Gail Higgins in obvious distress. She was huddled up on a stone step. The girl looked so sad and helpless that Sam was touched. She decided to find out what was wrong and went into the playground. As soon as Gail saw her coming, however, she shrunk away.

'Wassa marrer?' asked Sam.

'Nuthin'.'

'You been cryin'? Your eyes are all red.'

'I'll be OK.'

'Anythin' I can do, Gail?'

'No.'

'Are you sure?'

Gail stared up at her resentfully then she shot a look of hatred at Kevin. He was still hurtling around the yard. Sam seized on the clue at once.

'Kev been upsettin' you?' she said.

'Nor really.'

'Wor did 'e do?'

'It was nuthin'.'

'We'll see about thar.'

Sam marched off to the middle of the playground and grabbed her brother by the arm as he tried to run past.

Kevin was brought to a sudden halt and he complained bitterly.

'Leggo!'

'I wanna talk to you, Kev.'

'Thar 'urt,' he said, rubbing his arm.

'Wor 'ave you done to Gail?'

'Eh?'

'She's in a terrible state. Look at 'er.'

Kevin glanced across at the unhappy figure then shrugged.

'Girls are always cryin',' he noted contemptuously.

'I ber this is your fault,' she accused.

'No, iss nor!'

'Wor did you say to 'er?'

'Nuthin'!'

'Give me the truth!' insisted his sister. 'Or I'll shake it out of you.'

It was no idle threat. Kevin was a sturdy boy but he was no match for Sam when she was roused. He knew what it was like to be set on by his sister and he wanted to avoid it at all costs.

'I'm waitin',' said Sam impatiently.

'All I did was . . .'

'Go on.'

'Wor Dad said. About Mrs 'iggins in that pub.'

Sam was horrified. She grabbed him with both hands this time.

'You told Gail about *thar*?'

'Yeah. Wass wrong?'

'Iss cruel. Thass wass wrong. Iss cruel and nasty!'

'I was only teasin',' he claimed.

'Thar only makes it worse,' she said angrily. 'Honess, Kev. You got no concern for other people's feelin's. 'ow would *you* like to be teased about somethin' like thar?'

'Well . . .'

47

'Oo, I could strangle you!'

She shook him hard then threw him in the direction of his bag. He picked it up and strolled warily back towards her. Sam had finally managed to arouse his guilt. He did not dare to look across at Gail now.

'Juss wait till I get you 'ome!' warned Sam.

'Sorry.'

'Iss too late for thar, Kev.'

She led the way back to the gate with Kevin at her heels. He was cowed and sobered now. He knew what to expect when he got back to the flat and it was a daunting prospect.

'Doan worry!' Sam called to Gail. 'Ian'll be 'ere soon.'

But the girl did not even hear the words. She was still brooding about her mother.

The euphoria soon wore off. When break ended, Iggy was fired up to vandalize Lambo's car in some way. With the support of the other boys, he felt that anything was possible. Throughout the afternoon, however, his enthusiasm waned. The plan was fraught with all kinds of dangers.

What if he was caught? How could he possibly pay for any damage? Could he get sent to court? Would they expel him?

Cold fear set in long before the bell rang to end the school day. Iggy fought off his anxieties and told himself that Lambo deserved to have her car attacked. Besides, it was more than a simple act of revenge. It was a means of proving himself. Mark, Pug and Elroy had devised a test for him. If he failed, life at the Sin Bin would be intolerable. He had to go through with it to win their respect.

Basher threw them out on the stroke of four so that he could get across to Woodfield for the staff meeting. With the three older boys in tow, Iggy also hurried over to the main school.

'You're in luck, Ig!' observed Mark.

'Dead easy!' said Pug.

'Carn go wrong,' assured Elroy.

The staff car park was near the sheds where Iggy always left his bike. Lambo's vehicle was in the middle of a row that was furthest from the buildings. There would be plenty of cover for Iggy.

They lurked in the shadows while the other pupils came for their bikes. During the noisy exodus, Iggy took a closer look at the estate car to work out what he was going to do. It had an aerial which could be bent and gleaming paintwork that could be scored with a penknife. But he did not really want to do either. Something inside him was still urging him to respect other people's property. He wasn't an instinctive vandal.

'Stand by!' said Mark.

'Almost time,' added Pug.

Elroy hustled the last few bike owners out of the way then kept watch on the windows in the building. Mark and Pug patrolled either end of the car park as lookouts.

Iggy's mouth went dry. The palms of his hands became sticky. There was a tingling sensation around the back of his neck. All his energy seemed to drain away.

Elroy got a signal from the other boys. The coast was clear.

'OK, man!' he said. 'It's all yours!'

'Wor – now?' gulped Iggy.

'Action!'

Making an effort to pull himself together, Iggy trotted off towards the estate car in the back row. He looked around furtively to see if he was being watched. Apart from his three new friends, there was nobody. It gave him fresh heart.

When he got to the car, he ducked down between Lambo's vehicle and the Ford Sierra that stood next to it. Further along the line he could see Basher's old Vauxhall

Cavalier. Don Sheen's motorbike was parked at the very end of the row. He was an intruder. The best thing he could do was to get it over with as quickly as possible.

But something held him back. The car was in such perfect condition that it seemed unkind to damage it in any way. There was another deterrent. Iggy saw a round sticker in the side window with a wheelchair symbol on it. He did not know that Lambo was disabled in some way. It chastened him.

He was caught between two stools. His conscience would not let him go on but his fear would not let him give up. Mark, Pug and Elroy would never forgive him. He had come this far so he simply had to do something to appease them. His eyes roved frantically over the car and settled on the wheels.

That was it. He could let the tyres down.

Kneeling down, he got to work at once. He unscrewed the dust cap from one of the front tyres then used the end of his biro to depress the valve. There was a loud hiss and he was terrified that it would be heard. When he stole a glance around, however, there was nobody in sight, not even the three boys. That was odd.

Iggy carried on with his task. It took an age. The big tyre had been pumped up to a high pressure and there was a lot of air to release. Very slowly, the rubber began to sag beneath the weight of the car. When the whole vehicle was leaning over at a slight angle, he stopped and moved to the rear tyre on the same side. Once again, the air came out in a fierce hiss.

He was still on tenterhooks in case anyone came but he reassured himself with the thought that Mark, Pug and Elroy were keeping a lookout for him. They must have taken cover themselves. That was why he could not see them. If there was any danger, they would raise the alarm with a whistled signal. Iggy kept at it and a second tyre was squashed flat.

His instinct was to give up while he was winning but he knew that the boys would expect him to be thorough. He had to let down all four tyres. Lambo's car would then be undrivable.

He was kneeling by the third wheel when he heard the footsteps. Chancing a peek over the bonnet, he froze in horror. It was Charlie, the school caretaker. The burly figure was heading in his direction. It was as if Charlie knew he was there.

Dropping his pen in surprise, Iggy looked around for help. Where were the others? Why didn't they warn him about Charlie? Surely one of them could distract the caretaker in some way?

But Charlie came relentlessly on. He was a middle-aged man with a bald head and a florid face. He gave vandals very short shrift if he caught them. Charlie was just like Basher. Hit them first and ask questions afterwards.

Iggy was galvanized into life. Rising from his hiding place, he made a run for it towards the bike sheds.

'Hey!' yelled Charlie. 'Come back!'

The caretaker broke into a run but he had no chance of catching the boy. Despite his bulk, Iggy was racing along as if he had wings on his heels. He reached the sheds, unlocked his bike, jumped on to it and cycled madly out through the gate. By the time the panting Charlie got there, all he could see was a glimpse of Iggy as bike and rider merged with the traffic.

'Little bleeder!' he cursed.

Mark Stavros, Pug Anderson and Elroy Cooper came up.

'You're gettin' too slow, Charlie,' said Mark.

'We told you where 'e was,' added Pug. 'All you 'ad to do was nab 'im.'

'I know who he is,' growled the caretaker. 'We'll catch up with him. It was that fat kid in 4C.'

Charlie stalked off to the main building to report the outrage to the staff. The three boys grinned and looked over at Lambo's car. Iggy had done a good job on it. More important, he had made his escape when he was cornered. Maybe he was not such a wimp as they thought. He had got out of their trap.

They were impressed.

When she got back from school, there were always several chores waiting for Sam and she pitched straight into them. She washed the dishes, tidied the flat then fed the two goldfish. Kevin had already been given a severe shaking and sent off to his room in disgrace. As a further punishment, Sam refused to make him any tea. He could starve until his parents came home.

Their mother worked at a cinema in the city centre, selling sweets and popcorn to the dwindling band of patrons. She would not be back until mid-evening. Her husband was a postman. His day began very early but it was almost finished by noon. He spent most afternoons at the betting shop, called into the pub at opening time and drifted back about the same time as his wife.

It meant that Sam had to bear the brunt of the chores and act as a kind of second mother to Kevin. The role gave her many problems. Like today. She could not forgive her brother for what he had told Gail Higgins and she winced when she remembered how upset Gail had been. It preyed on her mind so much that she decided to take action.

Sam went over to pound on Kevin's door.

'I'm juss goin' out for a few minutes!' she said.

'Where?'

'Never you mind. Stay in there.'

'Bur I'm 'ungry,' he wailed.

'Thass your bad luck. Doan you dare leave thar room.'

'Wor about the telly?'

'You're nor seein' any tonight!'

'Aw, Sam!'

She left him squawking and went out. It was cold and dark outside and the lights on the steps did not really pierce the gloom. Sam ran up the eight flights then walked along the concrete balcony that fronted the flats. She came to a door and rang the bell.

There was a lengthy pause. Nobody came. Sam lifted the flap of the letterbox and called through it.

'Is anybody there?'

Iggy's voice sounded distant and very tentative.

'Who is it?'

'Me – Sam!'

'Oh.'

He came to open the door at once and stared at her in surprise. Though they lived in the same block of flats, they were not on calling terms. Her visit was most unusual.

'Can I come in?' she asked.

'Uh . . . yeah.'

'Freezin' out 'ere.'

She stepped in past him and he closed the door.

'Your mum back?' said Sam in an undertone.

'No. Why?'

'I need to speak to you on your own.'

'Me? Wor for?'

Iggy did not know whether to be pleased or disturbed. There was something about the girl's manner which suggested that it was not a social call.

'Where's Gail?' she whispered

'In the kitchen. 'aving her tea.'

'Good. I'll keep my voice down, then.'

Sam breathed in deeply. Whatever she had come for, it

was making her feel embarrassed. Eventually, she came out with it.

'I juss wanned to apologize.'

'Why?'

'For wor our Kev said to Gail.'

'Gail?' Iggy was baffled.

'Didden she tell you?'

'Tell me wor?'

'Oh dear!'

Sam's face crumpled. It was going to be even more awkward now. Iggy tried to explain his own movements.

'I was late pickin' Gail up at school,' he said evasively. 'She didden say a word. All she wanned was to get back 'ere quick. Wass this about your brother?'

There was no point in holding it back now. Sam moistened her lips with her tongue then blurted out the details.

'Kev told 'er somethin' he shudden,' she began. 'It was very wrong of 'im. Dad was to blame, really. He told us wor 'e saw in the pub and Kev 'eard. So Kev then goes and teases Gail abour it. I nearly pulverized 'im. Woan 'appen again.' She inhaled deeply once more. 'Wor Dad said was this. When 'e was down the pub, 'e saw your mum there with this . . . with this man, like. Thass all.'

It was enough to turn Iggy bright scarlet.

His traumatic day at the Sin Bin had pushed everything else out of his mind but other worries now returned to haunt him. The shock of finding that his mother had brought a man back to the flat was bad enough. It made him feel very confused. Sam's tale had made it all much worse. Other people *knew*. They were talking about his mother. He was speechless.

Sam could see his discomfort and was very sympathetic.

'Doan take it too 'ard, Ian,' she advised. 'It might nor mean anythin' at all. Forgerrit.'

But his mind was raging. How could he forget this?

'Right. Well . . . I berra go.'

Iggy opened the door and stood aside. Sam went out into the cold then turned back for a final word. Shaking her head, she heaved a sigh of regret.

'I'm sorry, Ian. So is Kev.'

Iggy nodded then closed the door. He could hear her footsteps retreating along the balcony. So much had happened to him in the past twenty-four hours. It was impossible to take it all in and to make sense of it. He was in a daze.

Wandering back into the living room, he was met by Gail.

'Who was thar?' she asked.

'Nobody.'

'I 'eard voices.'

'Someone called.'

'Who?'

'Sam Jarrett.'

The girl coloured immediately and swallowed hard. She did not need to say anything. Gail was not old enough to work out what was really going on but she had grasped one thing. Their mother lied to them. She did not go out for a drink with the other women from Sainsbury's. She had a special friend. A man.

'Ian . . .'

'Yeah?'

'Wor made Dad leave?'

'Dunno.'

'Will 'e ever come 'ome again?'

Before he could answer, the doorbell rang again. It made them both jump. He decided that it must be Sam again. She had come back to say something else. It had been very painful to talk to her about something so personal but one thing was clear. Sam cared about him. She was a real friend.

55

He opened the door and expected to see her face. But he was disappointed.

'Hello, Ian,' said a stern female voice. 'You and I need to have a little chat.'

He backed away in alarm. It was Lambo.

Chapter Six

The big advantage of living over a fish and chip shop was that Mark Stavros could have as many free meals as he could eat. As long as he chose them from the menu. The disadvantage was that he had to help out behind the counter now and again. It was hard work and the smell got into his clothes and hair. But the Stavros Fish Bar was a family business and they all had to do their share.

'Gimme one of them pies,' said Elroy.

'Steak and kidney or ham and mushroom?' offered Mark.

'Steak. There's more in 'em.'

Mark used a pair of metal tongs to lift the pie on to the pile of chips that already nestled in their greaseproof bag. He added liberal doses of salt and vinegar then scooped it all up in a sheet of paper and set it out on the counter. Elroy was going to eat it there and then. He tried a chip.

'Great!' he complimented.

'A Stavros special!' said Mark.

'Almost good enough to pay for!'

Neither Elroy nor Pug had to spend any money on their fare. As close friends of Mark and regular visitors, they got their meals free as well. Very occasionally, they too would take a turn behind the counter.

While Elroy took a first bite out of his pie, Pug was feeding coins into the fruit machine and pulling the handle with vicious intent. He made plenty of noise but won very little of his money back. It only drove him on to try again.

During the lull, Mark wiped the working surfaces with a damp cloth. Elroy spoke through a mouthful of pie.

'Wor 'appens next?'

'Eh?'

'To Iggy, I mean.'

'Thass up to us,' said Mark.

'Did well today. I gor admit 'e surprised me.'

'And me. Never thort he could run thar fast!'

'Charlie never gor near 'im.'

'So wor do we do?'

'Hooray!' cheered Pug as he finally struck gold.

Gathering up all the coins he had just won, he began to put them back into the machine. The deafening noise continued. Mark was still thinking about the latest recruit to the Sin Bin.

'Try 'im with somethin' bigger,' he decided.

'Think old Iggy is up to it?'

'Only one way to find out, El.'

'Wor we gonna do, then?'

'Take 'im along for the ride. Next time we . . .'

Mark broke off abruptly as his father came out of the living room to join him. Tony Stavros was a shorter, stouter, older version of his son. His temples were greying and he wore a moustache. Apart from that, he and Mark bore a striking similarity. Their white coats and aprons were identical.

Tony Stavros sensed what they had been talking about and he was uneasy. Unlike his son, he still had his heavy foreign accent. He flicked a pair of dark eyes at Mark.

'We don't want you getting into more trouble.'

'I know wor I'm doin', Dad.'

'Since when?'

'I do!'

'Is that why they keep you in this Sin Bin?'

'Mark is the best kid in the class,' said Pug.

'Yeah,' agreed Elroy. 'Good as gold, Mr Stavros. Smart, polite, well-behaved.'

'I believe it when I see it,' said Tony cynically.

'Doan be like thar, Dad.'

'Then keep out of trouble.'

'I try to.'

'Think of us for once. Don't let the family down.'

'Never dream of it,' said his son easily.

But Tony Stavros was not convinced. Mark and the others were problem kids at Woodfield. They had caused so much trouble that they were now more or less permanent residents at the Sin Bin. It was their home. Tony was very keen to do well in his adopted country. He worked long hours and was always friendly to his customers. The one thorn in his flesh was Mark.

'It's time for you to grow up, son.'

'Ger off my back, Dad, will you?'

'I'm only trying to help you.'

'I can take care of myself.'

Tony Stavros clicked his tongue in resignation. Picking up a large metal basket, he went out to get a fresh supply of potatoes. Mark pulled a face at Elroy.

'Juss as well 'e duzzen know wor *really* goes on!'

'Same with my old man,' said Elroy.

'Fathers are all alike.'

'Mine's nor,' argued Pug as he pulled the lever again. 'Duzzen care a monkey's about me. Still inside for thar ware'ouse job. Woan be out again for two years.'

Elroy put some chips into his mouth and munched away.

'Comin' back to Iggy . . .'

'Wor about 'im?' said Mark.

'Did you mean wor you was sayin' juss now?'

'Course. Less see wor 'e's made of, shall we?'

'Could be fun.'

'Oh, we 'aven't finished with Iggy yet.'

'Thass good news. Doan you agree, Pug?'

59

'Hurray!'

Pug Anderson was not listening. He had just hit the jackpot for the second time. His luck was changing.

Arms akimbo and feet planted well apart, Charlie stood over the miscreant and made sure that he did the job properly. He wanted no shirking.

'Harder!' he urged.

'I'm doin' my best,' gasped Iggy.

'You let 'em down. Now you pump 'em up again.'

'My legs are aching.'

'Something else'd be aching if it was left to me!'

Iggy thrust down rhythmically with his right foot and tried to ignore the pain. He was operating a foot pump so that he could inflate the tyres on Lambo's car again. She had hauled him out of his flat and taken him back to Woodfield. While he struggled away under the watchful gaze of the caretaker, Lambo sat in the driving seat and waited. It did not endear her to him.

As exhaustion threatened him, Iggy broke off.

'It must be 'ard enough now.'

'I'll check,' said Charlie, using a tyre gauge. 'Yes, that's close enough. Only one more to go.'

'Carn I 'ave a rest?' pleaded the boy.

'Not on your life!'

'Iss murder!'

'Shut your trap and start pumping.'

Iggy connected up the machine and started once more. He had learned one thing. It was far easier to let air out of a tyre than to pump it back in again. He forced himself on and the job was eventually done to the satisfaction of the caretaker.

'You're getting the hang of it now, son,' he said.

'My legs are droppin' off!'

'Know the moral of the story?'

'Doan ler people's tyres down.'

'No,' whispered Charlie. 'Don't get caught.'

Seeing that the work was all done, Lambo lowered the window and bestowed a thin smile on the caretaker.

'Thank you, Charlie.'

'All part of the service.'

'I must be off.'

She switched on the ignition and the engine came to life. Too tired to move, Iggy just stood there and gulped in air. Lambo beckoned him.

'Get in the car, Ian.'

'Me, miss?'

'Who else, boy? Come on. I'll drive you home.'

The threat made him very flustered.

'Er, no . . . thass OK, miss, bur I can walk. Snor far, like.'

'Get in,' she persisted. 'I *have* to go back to Clearview.'

'Why, miss?'

'So that I can talk to your mother.'

Iggy's stomach lurched. Things were just getting worse. Lambo was going to tell on him. She wanted his own mother to gang up against him. Two women who alienated him.

With great reluctance he got into the car and put on the safety belt. Both his legs were throbbing now and it was a relief to sit down but he would not admit that. Iggy would rather have pumped up another three tyres than have to share a car ride back home with Lambo. She was deadly poison.

The car moved forward and soon joined the road.

'How do you think she will take it?' asked Lambo.

'Who, miss?'

'Your mother. How will she react when she hears what you did to my car?'

'She woan like it,' confessed Iggy.

'Neither did I! Whatever possessed you to do it?'

'Dunno, miss.'

'It was fortunate that the caretaker saw you at it,' she continued. 'Otherwise, I might never have known. I'd have had to call the AA. Didn't you consider all that when you let down my tyres?'

'No, miss.'

'What *is* wrong with you, Ian?'

'Nothin', miss.'

'Maybe your mother can provide the answer.'

'She woan be there, miss,' he lied.

'Then I will wait until she comes back,' vowed Lambo. 'However long it takes. I simply must speak with her. And with your father.'

'You carn talk to Dad, miss.'

'Why not?'

'Because he's gone away.'

'Where?'

'Dunno, miss. Juss away.'

June Higgins was in a bad temper. She came home to find Gail had been left in the care of a neighbour so that Iggy could go back to school. She was furious.

Lambo arrived with Iggy and asked for the opportunity to chat with his mother. June agreed and quickly cleared away a pile of magazines from the sofa. She knew it would be important if one of the teachers had actually brought her son home. Iggy was sent off to his room so that the women could talk in peace. It made him feel even more cut off. Decisions about his life were being made in the next room and he wasn't even allowed to hear them.

What he did hear was the steady buzz of conversation and the clink of teacups. The sounds went on for quite some time then Lambo took her leave. June called Iggy out. She was bewildered as much as annoyed.

'Why didden you tell me about it?' she demanded.

'About wor?'

'All this. Bein' cheeky in class to Mrs Lambert. Startin' a fire. Goin' to the Sin Bin.'

'Didden think you'd be interested.'

'I'm your mother, Ian. Of course I'm interested. I've a right to know.'

'You do now.'

'I'd rather 'ave 'eard it from you.'

'Bur I never ger the chance to talk to you.'

'Of course you do. I'm around every day.'

'No, Mum. You're always doin' somethin' else.'

June Higgins was thrown on the defensive.

'If you mean last night,' she said hotly, 'thass my business. I'm entitled to 'ave a drink with a friend and I woan be made to feel guilty.'

'Who is 'e?' asked Iggy without enthusiasm.

'His name is Rob Ford. Lives nearby.'

Iggy recognized the name. It was painted on the side of a transit van that parked in the next street. Rob Ford was a plumber. And he was definitely younger than Mrs Higgins.

'Will you be seein' 'im again?'

'Yes,' she retorted. 'Often. You'll get used to it.'

'Wor about Dad?' asked the boy wistfully.

'Wor about 'im?'

The conversation had reached a stone wall. June was obviously not prepared to say any more. Iggy was being kept at arm's length once again. He withdrew into himself and went off to his bedroom. It had been a truly terrible day.

There was plenty for him to brood about as he lay in the darkness that night. Did his father leave of his own accord or was he driven away? How long had his mother known Rob Ford? Was he the real reason why Vance Higgins went away? Where would it all end? Who could Iggy turn to for help?

He felt lonely, rejected and beset by enemies. It was well past midnight before he finally fell asleep.

The Sin Bin was created to frighten pupils back into line. Four main elements moulded its regime. There was constant supervision, iron discipline, total loss of privileges and unremitting work. Since the man in charge was Basher Bowen, a certain amount of recreation was allowed but he made sure that nobody enjoyed it.

'Keep going!' he bellowed.

'Aw, sir!'

'Carn go any further!'

'Iss rainin'!'

'Less go back, sir!'

'One more circuit!' ordered Basher. 'Don't stop.'

He had taken his class to the nearby park and was forcing them to run around its perimeter. They puffed their way along while he rode behind them on a bicycle. Rain only added to their problems. They were soon soaked to the skin.

Mark Stavros was the only one who did not mind the extended run. Covering the ground with long, loping strides, he was well ahead of the field. Elroy Cooper came next, bounding along like a jack rabbit but gradually running out of steam. Pug Anderson was no athlete. He lumbered along towards the rear and cursed Basher under his breath.

Iggy was right at the back, plodding along in agony but determined not to show it. The Dean of Discipline lashed him unmercifully with his tongue.

'Run, boyo!' he roared. 'Shift that fat carcass of yours! Look at you wobbling along! Like a strawberry jelly with legs!'

The abuse kept Iggy on the move all the way round. Over the closing stages, Basher cycled alongside him so that he could yell right into the boy's ear.

'Let's have that finishing burst, mun! See if you can run the last fifty yards in under four minutes! Come on! You're slower than a three-legged tortoise! Give it all you got!'

Spurred on by the Welshman, Iggy found a spurt of sorts and actually managed to overtake Pug. The two of them almost collapsed when they stopped running.

Hands on knees, they bent double and gasped for breath.

'Bellows to mend!' said Basher. 'You're not fit!'

'Why carn we play soccer instead?' asked Elroy.

'Because that might be fun, boyo. You're here to *suffer*!'

He led the way back to the Sin Bin. They staggered along behind him and ignored the gibes he kept throwing over his shoulder. Mark, Pug and Elroy fell in alongside Iggy. It was the first chance they had had to discuss the sabotage of Lambo's car.

'That was rotten luck last night, Ig,' said Mark.

'Trust Charlie to turn up and spoil it,' added Elroy.

'We 'ad to beat it before he cort us as well,' explained Pug. 'We tried to warn you, like, but you didden see us.'

'You did juss great,' praised Mark.

'Thanks,' said Iggy.

'Pity old Lambo made you pump up 'er tyres again.'

'Yeah.'

'Must've been 'ard work.'

'Torture.'

'We'll be more careful next time.'

'Next time?' repeated Iggy.

'You carn juss leave it there,' argued Mark.

'No,' said Elroy persuasively. 'You gor even more reason to ger back at Lambo now. And not only 'er.'

Pug indicated Basher. 'There's 'im as well.'

'And Froggie Parsons,' said Mark.

Iggy nodded in agreement. He had no love for Wood-field's headmaster. First thing that morning, Froggie summoned him for interview and harangued him for what he did in the car park. Iggy's reward was a longer sentence. He was stuck in the Sin Bin until further notice.

It was not fair. It made his blood boil.

'Mark's gor this ace plan, like,' said Elroy.

'Wor is it?' asked Iggy.

'Iss top secret,' Pug told him.

'Juss a few more details to work out,' said Mark. 'You interested?'

'Yeah,' replied Iggy with slight hesitation.

'We only wann you if you're dead keen,' warned Mark.

'You woan do nuthin' on your own this time,' assured Elroy. 'We'd be with you all the way, like. Iss a fantastic idea.'

'Carn fail,' muttered Pug, scratching his stomach.

They gave Iggy a few moments to think it over. It did not take him long to reach a firm decision. He hated Woodfield now. If there was a plan to strike back at Froggie Parsons, Lambo, Basher and all the rest of them, then he wanted to be involved in it. Iggy cast his vote.

'Count me in!'

They patted him on the back and welcomed him. Iggy felt like a member of the gang. It gave him a surge of power.

'Count me in!' he repeated. 'I'll do anythin'!'

He would wish he'd never said that.

Chapter Seven

Mrs Lambert was a creature of habit. She had been at Woodfield for over ten years now and had settled into a regular routine. At the end of each day, when she had checked that everything was in order in the science laboratory, she would go down to the staff room for a cup of tea. It had to be brewed exactly right. Dark and stewy with a touch of milk and two artificial sweeteners. She would then sit in her special chair and have a natter with some of her older colleagues. They, too, needed a restorative drink after another taxing day at Woodfield.

The well-established Lambo routine was upset that day. Someone was actually sitting in her chair. She was about to complain when he stood up to greet her.

'Hello, Mrs Lambert.'

'Mr Sheen . . .'

'Hope you don't mind,' said Don. 'I dashed over from the Annexe to see if I could catch you.'

'Me?' She was surprised.

'Yes. Er . . . shall we take a pew?'

He was about to lower himself down again when he saw a glint in her eye. Lambo was very territorial. It was much wiser to let her have her own chair. He stood aside to let her sit down then perched on the edge of a chair opposite her.

'This won't take long, Mrs Lambert.'

'I see.'

'You can guess why I'm here.'

'Not really, Mr Sheen.'

In the normal course of events, they hardly ever saw

each other. They were in different departments and had very little in common. Don was put off by her battleaxe image and Lambo distrusted him because he was so earnest. Also, he was dishevelled. That counted against him. She was always impeccable.

'It's Ian Higgins,' he said.

'Oh dear!'

'Fascinating case.'

'Really?' She sipped her tea.

'He doesn't belong with us at all.'

'At the Annexe, you mean?'

'The Sin Bin is for real boat-rockers.'

'Ian Higgins can rock a boat when he wants to,' she noted with some asperity. 'He let down the tyres on my car yesterday.'

'That was afterwards, Mrs Lambert.'

'Afterwards?'

'He'd never have done it before.'

'You're not making much sense, Mr Sheen.'

'Sorry. All I'm saying is that Ian Higgins would never have thought of touching your car. Then he got sent to us. He knows that only troublemakers come to the Sin Bin so he takes on the protective colouring of the place. *He* makes trouble.'

'I'm not sure that I go along with that.'

'It's only a theory.'

'Ah. Do you know why he chose *my* car?'

'I think so. You're the focus.'

'For what?'

'All his anger and distress.'

'But why me?'

'Because you got him sent to the Annexe.'

'I had to,' she argued. 'He started a fire in the lab.'

'That was a cry for help, Mrs Lambert.'

'I know flames when I see them.'

'Ian didn't mean any harm.'

'Oh, I see. And I suppose he didn't mean to let down my tyres either. Was that another cry for help?'

'In a way.'

'I take the old-fashioned view, Mr Sheen. When children misbehave, you have to come down on them. Give them an inch and they'll take a mile. Discipline is the only answer.'

'You sound like Basher,' he murmured.

'I beg your pardon?'

'Nothing . . . What interests me about Ian is this . . .'

'Do we have to continue this discussion?' she asked with cold politeness. 'We're never going to agree. That's obvious.'

'One last point.'

She sighed. 'All right, then.'

'This anger. I think I know the cause of it.'

'He obviously doesn't like me.'

'It's nothing to do with you, Mrs Lambert.'

'Now, come on!'

'It isn't. The lad has domestic problems. From what I can make out, his father's left home. Ian idolized him. They used to go to soccer matches together and all that. Dad goes and so do all the good times. He has no idea what's hit him. I dare say he blames his mother for what happened. The anger is swirling around inside him. It came out that day in the science lab.'

'Thank you for telling me.'

'There's no need to be sarcastic, Mrs Lambert.'

'I just want to drink my tea in peace.'

'What about the kid?' he demanded.

'What about him?'

'Don't you *care*?'

'Calm down, Mr Sheen.'

'Honestly!' he exclaimed, jumping to his feet. 'You're as

69

bad as Mr Parsons. You think you can just sling kids in the Annexe and forget about them. Out of sight, out of mind. Ian Higgins is a human being, you know. OK, he stepped out of line and you came down on him like a ton of bricks. That doesn't mean we write him off. You've seen him. He's in pain. Doesn't that matter to you?'

Before she could answer, he stalked out of the room.

Lambo was taken aback. Nobody had ever talked to her like that. Least of all a young teacher with much less experience than she had. Don Sheen had behaved very rudely. She would tell him so the next time she saw him. He had ruffled her.

He had also made her think. As she sipped her tea and reflected, she thought about the mean flat in Clearview and the talk she had had with June Higgins. It was certainly not a happy home. She could feel the tension there. Don Sheen had caught her on the raw but he had proved one thing.

Lambo did care about Ian Higgins. A lot.

Samantha Jarrett pushed her brother in through the gate at Cameron Road Junior School then set off in the direction of Woodfield. It was her best day of the week. Double English in the morning. Her favourite subject. Games in the afternoon. She captained the hockey team and was an excellent player. Sam walked along with a spring in her step. When she heard the whirr of bicycle wheels, she glanced around. Iggy was approaching.

'Hello!' she called with a wave of the hand.

'Hello.'

'You in a rush?' she asked.

'No. Why?'

'Walk with me. Borin' on my own. Nice to 'ave company.'

Iggy did not need to be asked twice. He dismounted

70

from his bike then wheeled it along beside her. He noted the hockey stick jutting out of her bag.

'Games?'

'If the weather stays dry.'

'Basher 'ad us out runnin' in the rain yesterday,' he moaned. 'Almost killed us. We done five miles.'

'I 'ate cross country.'

'This was in the park.'

Iggy was delighted to be strolling along with Sam. When he first saw her, he intended to cycle past her but her friendly invitation had stopped him. She was not like the other girls. They giggled all the time and made silly remarks. Sam was more relaxed and grown-up somehow.

'We 'eard about Lambo's tyres,' she said.

'Oh, yeah.'

'I'd love to've seen 'er face when she found out! I ber she wenn up the flippin' wall. Wor did she say to you?'

'You know Lambo.'

He pulled a face and they both laughed.

'Shame old Charlie spotted you.'

'It was worth it,' he boasted.

'Wor did it feel like?'

'Bit scary at first.'

'Bur exciting, like?'

'Fantastic!'

'Wish I could play a joke like that on 'er. Must be great.'

'It was. Until Lambo came after me.'

'Was it a shock when she turned up at the door?'

'Yeah. Much rather *you* rang our bell.'

It was a clumsy compliment but she accepted it with a smile. They walked on side by side until the school came into view. The further they went, the more at ease Iggy became. Sam was fun. She was also a very sensitive girl. She made no mention of Mrs Higgins and a large area of potential embarrassment vanished. All she wanted to hear about were the rigours of the Sin Bin.

'Dunno 'ow you stand it, Ian.'

'Iss nor bad.'

'Do the others push you around?'

'Nor any more. They knows me berra now.'

'So do I.'

She flashed him a smile.

They were close to Woodfield now and were caught up in the hordes that milled around. Some girls from 4C joined them, shot admiring glances at Iggy, then bore Sam away with them. She waved goodbye to him and called above the clamour.

'See you at Cameron Road.'

Iggy hurried on to the bike sheds, chained his machine then went back towards the main entrance. A number of his classmates exchanged greetings with him as he went past. The Sin Bin gave him lustre. They all wanted to talk to him now.

He crossed the road and hurried on down to the Annexe. It was almost eight-thirty and Basher was strict about punctuality. Iggy made it with a couple of minutes to spare.

Pug Anderson was waiting for him inside.

'Saw you with thar girl,' he observed.

'Wor?'

'Sam Jarrett. 4C.'

'We was juss . . . walkin' along, like.'

'You goin' steady with 'er, then?'

'No!' denied Iggy. 'She lives in Clearview, thass all.'

'Good.'

'Why?'

'Fancy 'er a bit myself,' said Pug off-handedly.

'Oh.'

'Do me a favour, will you, Ig?'

'Wass that?'

'Arsk 'er if she'll go out with me, like.'

'Carn you speak to Sam yourself?'

'You knows 'er berra. OK?'

Iggy was in a quandary. While he was not Sam's boyfriend, he did not want to find one for her. Especially if it was Pug. He was an unappealing youth at the best of times. The thought of him and Sam together made Iggy shiver slightly.

'Will you 'ave a word with 'er?' urged Pug.

'If you like.'

'Ta, mate.'

He took out some chewing gum and handed a stick of it to Iggy. Though he was trying to be cool about it, Pug was desperate to have a girlfriend of his own. Since he could not get one for himself, he was having to use a go-between. It was a role that Iggy would not enjoy playing.

'Sam Jarrett,' mused Pug. 'Nice little piece!'

Iggy wished it could have been any other girl.

Froggie Parsons paid one of his rare visits to the Annexe that morning. The Sin Bin was very much his creation but he usually gave it a wide berth. He was content to leave the pupils there to the not-so-tender mercies of Basher Bowen. Froggie's only concern was to get any disruptive influences out of the main school.

He made an identical speech to both classes. It was a combination of threat, promise and muddled educational theory. Don Sheen cringed every time he heard it but Basher was more receptive to the sentiments expressed. As the headmaster spoke to his class, the beefy Welshman stood by the door like a bouncer at a disreputable nightclub.

Froggie bunched his fist to pound the table for effect.

'Make no mistake about it!' he thundered. 'I've tamed

tougher schools than Woodfield and I'll tame you. We set high standards of behaviour. Because you fail to reach those standards, you've been put in the Annexe for special treatment . . .'

Basher chuckled quietly. *He* was the special treatment.

'I have no illusions,' continued Froggie, adjusting his spectacles. 'I do not expect every child to be an angel. I do not ask for whiter-than-white purity. But I will not put up with lying, deception, bullying and petty theft. That is why most of you are here. You have forfeited your right to share in the privileges of the main school. You are outcasts. It's up to you to show that you're keen to come back to us. Play by our rules and you can't go wrong. Buck the system and you stay here.'

The speech was over. He nodded complacently to Basher.

'Any questions for Mr Parsons?' asked the other.

Dead silence. Froggie surveyed the thirteen faces.

'Isn't there anything you want to know?'

'Yeah, sir,' said Mark.

'Well, Stavros?'

'When do we break up?'

Suppressed laughter rumbled. Mark collected a glare from Basher for asking such a facetious question. Froggie pointed a finger at him.

'Stavros is a symbol of youth today,' he announced. 'He is a perfect example of waste. He is able, intelligent and has everything going for him. But he throws it all away. What a shameful denial of his talent. He is wasting his life here.'

'We all are, sir,' quipped Mark.

'Belt up!' shouted Basher.

'Stavros is a lost soul,' resumed Froggie. 'Make sure the rest of you don't catch his disease.'

'What's he gor, sir?' asked Elroy. 'Aids?'

'Watch it, Cooper!' boomed the Dean of Discipline.

Froggie struck an attitude to deliver his last line.

'Be warned. The name Stavros means only one thing.'

'Fish and chips,' said Mark.

Even Basher took time to quell the mirth.

When the class finally settled down, the Welshman set them some work and conducted the headmaster out. As they parted at the front door, Froggie was in a cheerful mood.

'I think that went down rather well, Bryn.'

'Er . . . yes, headmaster.'

'My little pep talks are so important to them. I do not mince my words but, at the same time, I offer them hope.'

'Is that what it is?'

'Punishment leavened with compassion,' asserted Froggie. 'That's what the Annexe is all about. I carry a stick in one hand and an olive branch in the other.'

'Very appropriate.'

Froggie took his leave and scampered across the road. Basher rolled his eyes in despair. No wonder Woodfield was such a dreadful school.

Wrapped up in her scarf and anorak, Gail Higgins kept close to her brother as they made their way past the shop windows. Most places were just closing and the last customers were being shown out. Gail paused to stare longingly at a doll in a toy shop.

'Come on,' said Iggy.

'Juss a minute.'

'You're too old for dolls.'

'No, I'm nor.'

'Anyway, we carn afford it.'

'I can still look.'

Iggy was worried about his sister. She hadn't recovered from the shock of what Kevin Jarrett told her in the playground. It made her morose and withdrawn. He could hardly get a word out of her. To cheer her up, he had offered to take her into the city. Instead of waiting for their mother to come home, they would meet her outside the supermarket.

When she had stared her fill, Gail turned away from the window and they headed up through the precinct. She lapsed back into a sullen silence again. Iggy did his best to draw her out.

'Wor was school like today?'

'Same as always.'

'See Mandy?'

'Yeah.'

'Why doan you arsk her round to play any more?'

'Mum woan lemme.'

'Oh.'

They came out of the precinct and went down the gradient towards Sainsbury's. It was on a corner near some traffic lights. Customers were dribbling out with bulging plastic bags. A security man was at the main door to stop anyone else going in.

June Higgins would have finished now. When her till roll had been checked against her cash receipts, she would be free to leave. All she had to do then was to change out of her overall. She didn't know the children were coming to meet her. Iggy hoped that she would be pleased.

That hope was stillborn.

He put a hand on Gail's shoulder to halt her.

'Wass wrong?' she said.

'Maybe this is nor such a good idea.'

'Wor d'you mean?'

'Mum might nor wann us to meet 'er.'

'Course she will!'

'Less go back,' suggested Iggy.

'Thass stupid. We come all this way.'

'I gorra think abour it.'

He held his ground as he wrestled with a problem.

Iggy had seen something which made his stomach turn. A transit van had pulled up on the double yellow line opposite Sainsbury's. He could guess the name on the side of the vehicle.

Rob Ford. Plumber.

Their mother did not need them. Someone was already meeting her.

Chapter Eight

Mark Stavros and Lynne Weller were the first to arrive at the cinema. They went into the foyer to get warm and to wait for the others. Lynne was one of the girls from the Sin Bin. She was tall, thin and rangy, with short fair hair. Lynne looked pleasant rather than pretty but she knew how to use make-up. Long earrings dangled down and trembled every time she laughed. Mark had taken her out a few times already.

'So wenn's this big night?' she asked.

'That'd be tellin'.'

'Who'll be there?'

'Pug, Elroy. One other, maybe.'

'Iggy?'

'Mind your own business,' he teased, slipping an arm around her waist. 'Less you know, the berra.'

'Why carn I come with you?'

'Cos we doan wann girls.'

'Thass nor wor you said Saturday night,' said Lynne with a giggle. 'Lemme come along as lookout or thar.'

'No. Men only.'

The door swung open and Elroy Cooper escorted in Ruth Wilson. They had been going out together for over six months and were very much at ease with each other. Ruth was a beautiful black girl with a big smile. Like Lynne, she wore a loose-fitting dress under her fashion coat.

Ruth ran an eye over the three choices available.

'Wor we gonna see, then?'

'James Bond,' decided Mark.

'Seen it before,' complained Lynne.

'Twice,' said Elroy. 'Been on the telly.'

'I fancy this one about Vietnam,' offered Ruth.

'Oo, no!' protested Lynne. 'Iss too bloodthirsty.'

'You'll 'ave to 'old on tight to Mark,' suggested Elroy.

'I'll do thar anyway,' promised the girl.

Her shriek of laughter made her earrings vibrate madly.

'I can guess wor film Elroy'd like,' said Mark. 'The new Eddie Murphy.'

'Gorrit in one, man!'

'Be worth a giggle,' agreed Lynne.

'I still say Vietnam,' maintained Ruth.

'Nor a chance, love,' said Elroy.

'Why nor?'

'No smokin'. Thar's no good to us.'

They continued to debate the possibilities. By the time that Pug Anderson arrived, they had still not decided on a film. Pug nodded a welcome to the others.

'On your own again?' mocked Elroy.

'You'll 'ave to join one of them computer datin' things, mate,' said Mark. 'They'll fix you up with someone.'

'I gorra girl,' claimed Pug.

'Who is she?' asked Elroy. 'The Invisible Woman?'

'Cudden come tonight, thass all.'

'Anyone we know?' wondered Lynne.

'Wait and see,' returned Pug with confidence.

'You serious?' challenged Mark.

'Why nor?'

'I think he means it,' said Elroy.

'Tell us 'er name,' urged Ruth.

'She at Woodfield?' probed Lynne.

'Yeah.'

Their curiosity was aroused. Pug had never managed to attract any girl before. They were dying to know who she was. He enjoyed their interest but refused to come up with a name.

'I'll bring 'er along next time,' he vowed.

With a little help from Iggy.

Rob Ford was making an effort to be nice but he was obviously irritated by them. He had been forced to give the children a lift back to Clearview when they showed up outside Sainsbury's to meet their mother. They got their first proper look at Rob. He was not at all like their father. Vance was a big, brawny, overweight man with a shock of ginger hair. Rob Ford had thick black hair and a dark complexion. His eyebrows met in the middle to form a single line. He was well-built and of medium height. He was still in his working clothes.

June Higgins invited him up to the flat and they had tea together. It was uncomfortable for all of them. June was eager for them to like her friend but they obviously did not. Rob was anxious to be alone with her and not have to bother with two children. Iggy was subdued and resentful. Gail was overwhelmed.

Leaving Iggy to wash up the tea things, June changed and did her make-up. Rob was at his most lively when he was leaving.

'Nice to meet you both,' he said, forcing a grin.

Iggy managed a polite nod but Gail just glowered at him.

'Say goodbye to Rob,' prompted their mother.

'Bye,' muttered Gail.

'Yeah,' said her brother.

'Doan stay up late,' cautioned June.

'Wenn will you be back?' asked Gail.

'Dunno.'

'Less go, June,' said Rob firmly. 'I gorra get changed.'

She made a show of kissing the children then followed him out. Their footsteps sounded on the concrete outside.

Gail looked crushed. She turned to Iggy.

'I doan like 'im.'

Her brother put the tea things into the sink and ran some hot water on to them. He added some washing-up liquid then made a start on the chore.

'I thort 'e was nasty,' admitted Gail. 'Who is 'e?'

'A friend.'

'Wor sort of friend?'

It was a question that Iggy had been asking himself all the time that Rob was there. He did not like the answer he was getting. The plumber had been on his best behaviour with them but he had spoken very familiarly to their mother. What shook Iggy was how much younger than her he was. Now that he had been able to study him, he guessed that there must be at least a ten-year age gap. He could not understand why this disturbed him so much.

'Ian . . .'

'Yeah?'

'Is 'e the same one?'

'As wor?'

'You know . . . Kevin Jarrett said thar – '

'Iss the same one,' confirmed Iggy.

He washed the dishes noisily and then dried his hands on a tea towel. Gail was now in the living room, staring vacantly at a television serial. He paced restlessly up and down as he tried to come to terms with what had happened.

His mother was to blame. When his father had been there, the place was always full of laughter and fun. At least, that was how he chose to remember it. But June Higgins drove her husband away. In no time at all, she had found someone else. A sudden thought pierced Iggy like a poisoned arrow.

Was she going to *marry* Rob Ford?

Where would that leave them?

Iggy broke out into a cold sweat and he became even more restive. After prowling the living room again, he moved to the door.

'I'm goin' out.'

'You carn leave me on my own!'

'I woan be far away, Gail. Gorra call to make.'

'Where?'

'On the ground floor. You stay 'ere.'

He took his key but scorned a coat. The chill night air was refreshing but it did not stop the drum that was now beating inside his head. Rob Ford's visit was significant in two ways. It showed that June liked him enough to introduce him to her children, and it set the seal on the departure of Vance Higgins. Their father was not coming back.

The drum was beating more loudly.

When he got to the ground floor, he made his way to the Jarrett flat and banged the knocker. The door opened after a few moments and Sam looked out at him. Her smile was spontaneous.

'Hello!'

'Hello . . .'

'Wassen expectin' visitors.'

'Gorra minute?'

'Yeah. Come in.'

Her parents were not home yet. Kevin Jarrett was glued to the television and did not even see them go past him into the kitchen. Sam closed the door behind them to shut out the noise.

'Kev is telly mad.'

'So's Gail.'

'Wor d'you watch, Ian?'

'Soccer, mostly. Films and thar. Oh, and the snooker.'

'I like snooker as well.'

'Who's your favourite?'

82

'Steve Davis.'

'I prefer Jimmy White.'

Sam glanced across at the kettle.

'Like a coffee or somethin'?'

'No thanks. Juss 'ad tea.'

An awkward silence followed. Iggy did not know how to break it. Sam tried to help him.

'Big surprise. You knockin' on our door.'

'Yeah.'

'Thort you were too shy for thar.'

'I am, really.'

A hint of a smile flitted across his lips.

'Wor brought you down this time, then?

'Pug.'

'Who?'

'Pug Anderson. Kid from 5B.'

'I know 'im,' she said with mild disgust.

'He's in the Sin Bin with me.'

'Best place for 'im. Wass 'e want?'

'Thing is . . .' The words dried up again. He had to force them out. 'Thing is . . . Pug saw us this mornin' . . . you know . . . we was walkin' together, like . . . Pug saw us . . .'e asked me if . . . if . . . I told him no . . . then 'e . . . Thing is . . .'

Sam Jarrett supplied her own translation at once.

'Pug fancies me.'

'Thass it.'

'So he made you arsk me if I'd go out with 'im.'

'Yeah.' His face clouded. 'Will you?'

'No!'

'Good.'

'I wouldn't go out with 'im if 'e was the only boy in the school – and you can tell 'im I said so!' She worked herself up into a rage. 'Pug's gorra damn cheek to make you do the arskin' for 'im. I ber 'e was afraid to do it 'imself. I

83

could never bother with anyone like thar. Pug Anderson is rude, ugly, smelly, ignorant and covered in spots. Ugh!'

'I'll juss tell 'im you said no,' decided Iggy.

'Say thar I doan go out with *any* boys,' she explained. 'I like to be friends with boys bur nor in thar way. And certainly not with the Monster of 5B!'

They shared a laugh. It helped Iggy to relax.

'I 'oped you'd say thar,' he admitted.

'I'd say a lot more if 'e was 'ere now. Apart from anythin' ele, iss nor very flatterin' to be so far down the list.'

'Wor list?'

'Doan you know?'

'Tell me.'

'Pug's tried everybody,' she said. 'He's already worked his way through the fifth year. No luck there at all. Now iss our turn. I reckon I'm about the sixth in our class.'

'Eh?'

'Iss the truth, Ian. Pug's love life is one big joke.'

Iggy grinned broadly. He had never liked Pug and now he had a weapon to use against him. The muscle man of the Sin Bin was a complete flop with the ladies. Most important of all, Sam did not like him. That filled Iggy with relief.

As soon as he dismissed Pug from his mind, however, Rob Ford came swimming back into it. Sadness returned. The pangs began to assail him once more.

Sam noticed the change in his manner.

'Anythin' up?'

'Nor really.'

'Is it your mum?'

Iggy nodded. He wasn't going to give any details. Sam did not press him for any. She showed her friendship in another way.

'I been thinkin' abour it . . .'

'Wor?'

'Your dad leavin'. There's a chance to ger in touch.'

'Is there?' he asked eagerly.

'Yeah. You know the firm 'e drives for, doan you?'

'Barrington's.'

'Ring 'em up,' she advised.

'Why nor?' he said as the penny dropped.

'They're bound to 'ave the new address.'

'I never thort of thar!'

'Juss as well you gor me, then.'

'Thanks, Sam! Iss a marvellous idea!'

He could not get over the simplicity of it. With one suggestion, she had dispelled his gloom completely. All was not lost. If he could make contact with his father, he was sure that he could persuade him to come home again.

Sam Jarrett really was a very special friend.

It was almost midnight when they carried out their reconnaissance. They approached the school from the back so that they would not have to go past the caretaker's house. His big Alsatian would be prowling around in the front garden. It was a vicious dog as more than one nocturnal visitor to Woodfield had found out.

They worked their way around to the dining hall which was a single-storey building. It did not take them long to shin up the drainpipe to get on to the flat roof. The dining hall was adjacent to the main building. Once on that roof, they would be away.

'Up you go, El.'

'You're a berra climber, Mark.'

'Juss gerrup there.'

He cupped his hands so that Elroy Cooper could put a foot in them. Stepping up, the West Indian reached for the parapet and got a firm grip. Mark gave him a final lift with his hands and Elroy hoisted himself up to the second roof. It was his turn to do the lifting now. Lying flat out, he

85

dangled an arm down from the parapet. Taking a little run at the wall, Mark got high enough to clasp the outstretched hand. Elroy took the strain. Mark used his friend's arm like a rope and pulled himself up until he got a purchase on the parapet. It was a matter of seconds to haul himself up on to the roof.

'Thanks, El.'

'You almost pulled my arm off.'

'We'll bring a rope next time.'

They were now on top of the main building. When they crept along to the far end and turned right, they were directly above the science block. They moved to the side along which the corridor ran. Set in the roof to give additional light was a series of circular windows the size of manholes. Thick, reinforced glass had been used. Elroy knelt down to examine the first window.

'We'd never break this, Mark.'

'Doan need to, mate. We unscrew it.'

'Dead clever!'

Five clamps held each window in place. Mark took a note of the size of the bolts that held them in position. He then stood up again and peered through the darkness.

'Wor you lookin' for?' asked Elroy.

'A way out.'

'We go down the way we gor up.'

'Yeah, bur we need a second escape route. Juss in case.'

'You think of everythin'.'

'Thass why I never get cort, El.'

Mark made a thorough search then settled on the water tank. It had stout iron struts at its base. They could easily tie a rope to it to make a speedy descent.

He recited all the things they would need.

'Two ropes. Spanners. Mole wrench. Torch.'

'Thar all?'

'We travel light, El.'

'Only one question left, then?'

'Wass thar?'

'Wenn do we do it?'

Mark weighed up all the factors involved.

'Saturday!'

'I'll be there!'

'Be like takin' candy from a baby!'

They were pleased with the night's work. Everything was in hand.

Don Sheen sat in the upstairs office at the Annexe and listened to a taped interview he had had with one of the pupils. It was the end of the day and he was puffing on his pipe as he relaxed with his feet up on the table. Everyone else had gone. He was alone in the building. Or so he thought.

There was a firm knock on the door.

Who is it?' he called.

The door opened and one of his colleagues swept in.

'It's me,' said Mrs Lambert.

Don was so surprised to see her that he almost fell off the chair. He quickly stood up and switched off the machine. The pupil's voice died in mid-sentence.

'Er . . . what can I do for you?' he wondered.

'How about starting with an apology?'

'Yes,' he conceded. 'I owe you that. Sorry, Mrs Lambert. I shouldn't have charged off the way I did. It was childish.'

'It was also unfair, Mr Sheen.'

'Unfair?'

'On both of us. You didn't get what you came for and I wasn't even allowed to give my point of view.'

'Fair comment.'

She lowered herself into a chair and smiled at him.

'Can I give you a piece of advice, young man?'

'I don't think I'll be able to stop you.'

'That's true,' she agreed. 'It's this. You catch more flies with honey than with vinegar. Take my point?'

'I think so.'

'If you're nice to people, they might co-operate. If you badger them, they'll probably give you the cold shoulder. Just as I did.' She became brisk. 'Right. Let's put all that behind us and begin again.'

'On what, Mrs Lambert?'

'Ian Higgins,' she said. 'You're right. The boy does need help. I want to pool our resources and see what we can do.'

'That's terrific!'

'No. It's just teaching.'

They were soon deep in discussion.

Chapter Nine

Iggy dropped his sister off at Cameron Road then lurked in a shop doorway for five minutes until Samantha Jarrett rolled up with her brother. It was worth the risk of being late to have her company on the way to Woodfield. Sam was pleased to see him again and anxious to know how he had got on.

'Did you pass my message on to Pug Anderson?'

'No.'

'Why nor?'

'Cos 'e was away yesterday.'

'As long as you gerrit across loud and clear.'

'I will,' he promised.

'Wor about thar phone call to Barrington's?'

'Cudden ger through, like.'

'Did you try more than once?'

'Five times,' he explained. 'From five different phone boxes. Three of 'em were vandalized. When I rang from the other two, the line was engaged.'

Sam could appreciate his dilemma. Locked up in the Sin Bin all day, he only had an hour or so in which to make his call. The Higgins family did not have a telephone so they had to rely on public call boxes. In an area like theirs, that was fatal. Most of the appliances had been damaged in some way.

'I'll have another go today,' he vowed.

'Isn't there a phone at the Annexe?'

'They'd never ler me use it.'

'Arsk,' she counselled. 'You could ger lucky.'

'Basher'd turn me down flat.'

'Then doan speak to 'im.'

'Eh?'

'Try Don Sheen instead. Softer touch.'

'Thass nor a bad idea,' he agreed.

'I do 'ave 'em now and again.'

They walked on amiably then turned in through the school gate. Sam was pounced on by her girlfriends and Iggy went off to park his bike. No sooner had he chained it up than he was accosted by the figure of Pug Anderson. He was anxious for news.

'Did you talk to 'er?'

'Yeah.'

'Wor did she say?'

'No deal.'

'You're lyin'!' exploded the other.

'Iss true, Pug,' said Iggy reasonably. 'Sam juss duzzen wanna go out with you.'

'Why nor?'

'She didden say.'

'Cos you never arsked 'er, thass why!'

'I did, honess!'

'Know wor I think, Ig?' said Pug menacingly. 'I think thar *you* fancy 'er as well. Thass why my message never gor through.'

'It did, Pug. She wassen interested, thass all.'

'I know a lie when I 'ear one,' snarled the bigger boy, grabbing Iggy and pinning him against the bike sheds. 'Now, tell me the truth or you'll gerrit.'

'I've *told* you the truth!'

Iggy tried to shake himself free but the other boy was far too strong. Just as he resigned himself to being thumped, he was rescued by Sam herself, who came scurrying on the scene.

'Leave 'im alone, you big ape!' she ordered.

'Yeah, yeah,' said Pug obligingly, releasing his victim.

'For the record, Ian did give me your invitation.'

'And?'

'Forgerrit!'

'Oh.'

'I wudden go out with you for all the tea in China!'

It was an unequivocal answer. Pug blinked a few times then lumbered off in a daze. One more name could be crossed off his list.

'Thanks, Sam.'

'Any time.'

Iggy waved goodbye and ran across to the Sin Bin, missing the full wrath of Basher Bowen by some thirty seconds. Everything was slotting nicely into place that morning.

There was also a welcome variation of timetable. In place of mindless copying out, they had a discussion on the extent of freedom in modern Britain. Basher was in the chair. When it was over, they had to write an essay on the subject.

Iggy was unable to concentrate. His mind kept returning to the phone call he had to make. It could be crucial. He simply had to track down his father.

When the lunch break came, he hurried upstairs and told his story to Don Sheen. The teacher was sympathetic.

'Glad to see you're taking the initiative, lad.'

'Thar mean I can use the phone?'

'Of course. In the office.'

'Ta, sir.'

'Put the catch on the door then you won't be disturbed.'

'Wor abour the money, like?'

'Have this one on us, Ian. It won't break the bank.'

Don unlocked the office then left Iggy alone to make his call. The boy fished into his pocket for a scrap of paper on which he had scribbled a number. He lifted the receiver and dialled slowly. There was a pause then the number rang out. His pulse quickened.

A woman's voice spoke at the other end of the line.

'Barrington's.'

'Er . . . wonder if you can 'elp me,' mumbled Iggy.

'Speak up, please. I can't hear you.'

Iggy cleared his throat and tried again.

'Iss abour my father.'

'Who?'

'My dad. 'e works there.'

'At Barrington's?'

'As a driver. 'iggins is the name. Vance 'iggins.'

'This is the administration office, sir. Your father is not on this number.'

'You doan understand,' asserted Iggy. 'I juss wanna know where 'e is.'

'I beg your pardon?'

'Gimme 'is address.'

'That's confidential information, I'm afraid.'

'Bur iss my dad!' he argued.

'It makes no difference, sir.'

'I gorra contact 'im. Urgent, like.'

'We can't release an employee's address to you.'

'*Please*!'

'I'm sorry, sir. Company policy.'

She put the receiver down and the line went dead.

High hopes had been dashed yet again. They were keeping his father away from him and there was nothing that he could do about it. He was plunged back into gloom.

As he left the office, Don was waiting for him.

'Any joy?'

'No, sir.'

'Wouldn't they give you the address?'

Iggy shook his head. The injustice of it all rankled.

'Some companies are a bit sticky about that kind of

thing,' said Don. 'We'll have to think of some other way. In the meantime, if ever you want to have a talk about it all . . .'

'No thanks, sir,' grunted Iggy.

'My door is always open.'

But Iggy was in no mood for conversation. After a hurt glance back at the office, he scuttled off downstairs. He was no nearer to finding his father. It was soul-destroying.

Froggie Parsons loved playing at being a headmaster. Though he took care never to teach a class himself, he enjoyed floating around the school and making unannounced visits to some of the lessons. He claimed that it kept him in touch with what was going on but his colleagues put another construction on it all. They felt he was spying on them and they resented the intrusion.

That afternoon found him wandering around the science block. After sitting through twenty minutes of a lesson on the nitrogen cycle, he strolled along to join a class that was being taken by Lambo. It was a model of precision. Keeping a firm control of her pupils, she demonstrated an experiment then got them to try it for themselves. With her guidance, they all did it right in the end.

When the bell went for break, Froggie lingered so that he could walk down to the staff room with her. He was complimentary.

'An excellent lesson, Mrs Lambert.'

'Thank you, headmaster.'

'You have such a feel for the subject.'

'I wish I could say the same for the children.'

'They can't all be first-rate chemists, alas!'

Reaching the ground floor, they strode along the corridor together. Lambo chose the moment to broach something that had been on her mind.

'I went over to the Annexe yesterday.'

'Indeed? Why?'

'Mainly because I'd never been there before. I wanted to see what the conditions are really like. Get some idea of the regimen.' Her jaw tightened. 'It was a trifle forbidding.'

'That is the intention, Mrs Lambert.'

'I know and I'm sure that it works for a certain type.'

'What do you mean?'

'I've been having second thoughts about Ian Higgins.'

'But the boy let down your tyres!'

'I may have over-reacted to that.'

'You had every right to,' he said airily. 'We can't condone that kind of behaviour at Woodfield.'

'But it's so untypical of the boy.'

'Makes no difference, Mrs Lambert. He must be punished.'

'The Sin Bin is not the right place for him.'

'Spare the rod and spoil the child.'

'There's such a thing as too much rod, headmaster.'

'I'm surprised to hear you – of all people – saying that. Discipline is at the heart of all teaching.'

They entered the staff room and joined the queue for tea or coffee. The place was buzzing with noise. Lambo had to raise her voice to speak above the din.

'I think there's a case for parole here.'

'For Ian Higgins?'

'Let him complete a week then haul him out.'

'But he's there until Christmas at least.'

'It'll be too late by then,' she warned. 'He'll have turned into a real problem.'

'He *is* a real problem. That's why he's there.'

'Mr Sheen takes my view.'

'I always rely on Mr Bowen's opinion,' overruled Frog-gie. 'He thinks that he can lick Higgins into shape and so do I. The boy stays at the Annexe.'

'There are domestic factors involved here.'

'There always are, Mrs Lambert. We've got more than our share of problem parents at Woodfield, believe you me. I never use them as an excuse for anti-social behaviour.'

'Is there no way you'll review this case?'

'Not until after Christmas.'

'The boy will have endured a lot of unnecessary suffering by then.'

'It will build his character.'

'Build it – or destroy it?'

But Froggie was no longer listening. He had reached the table and was involved with a much more important decision.

'Let me do the honours, Mrs Lambert,' he offered. 'Yours is tea, I know. I think I might join you. No – a coffee is called for, I fancy. Yes – one tea, one coffee. I've made up my mind.'

Lambo let out a quiet sigh. She had made her bid but she had failed.

There was no escape for Iggy. They followed him all the way to the bike sheds to hound him. He was no match for the three of them but he tried to argue his way out of it.

'You promised us, Ig!' reminded Mark Stavros.

'Yeah,' chipped in Elroy. 'You gave us your word, man.'

'Lost your nerve?' accused Pug.

'No,' said Iggy.

'Then stop messin' us about!' warned Mark.

'We doan like people who ler us down,' said Pug. 'Funny things 'appen to 'em. Know wor I mean?'

'I'm nor backing out!' urged Iggy.

'So why all this hassle?' asked Elroy.

'Because I carn make it on Saturday.'

'Why nor?' said Mark bluntly.

'Cos I gorra look after Gail.'

'We doan even meet until midnight,' argued Elroy. 'Your sister'll be farst asleep by then.'

'I'm supposed to stay there.'

'Why?'

'I am, thass all!'

'Wor about your mum and dad?' pressed Mark. 'Where will they be on Saturday night?'

'Duzzen marrer,' said Iggy evasively.

'Course it marrers. Where will they be?'

'Tell us!' threatened Pug.

Iggy bit his lip and paled under the interrogation. They would not let him go until he had given them some explanation.

'Dad is . . . workin' away,' he said.

'Workin' away or playin' away?' teased Elroy.

'Thar still leaves your mum,' noted Mark.

Iggy's discomfort increased. If he told them the truth, they would mock him cruelly. As it was, Elroy's guess was not all that wide of the mark.

'I reckon 'is mum's run off with the milkman.'

'Shurrup!' he snarled.

'Temper, temper!' said Elroy.

'I'm still waitin' for an answer,' said Mark.

'Mum will . . . be back very late,' muttered Iggy.

'Where from?' asked Pug.

'She's workin' as a stripper in a nightclub,' suggested Elroy with a wicked grin. 'Or maybe she works night shifts!'

'I carn come on Saturday!' repeated Iggy.

'You got no choice, mate,' said Pug with a sneer. 'We're nor gonna change things round juss to suit you.'

'No way!' reinforced Mark. 'There's a lorra work gone into this already and iss nor gonna be wasted. Me and Elroy did a first run to sort out all the details so it'll be easy when we do the job. Everythin's been set up. Now you wanna come along and alter it.'

'Why nor go without me?' pleaded Iggy.

'I knew it!' jeered Pug. "e's yellow!'

'No,' decided Elroy, adopting a more persuasive approach. 'Old Iggy's juss playin' 'ard to ger. I think 'e's 'oldin' out for a bigger share of anythin' we nick.'

'I'm nor. You lor can 'ave it all!'

'Big deal!' said Pug.

'Sorry,' apologized Iggy. 'Saturday is juss impossible.'

Mark Stavros had heard enough. He stood very close to Iggy so that their faces were almost touching. His voice was quiet and measured but all the more menacing for that.

'Lemme spell it out for you, Ig,' he explained. 'We gor the idea and you bought into it. Right? You carn juss drop out when you fancies. We need you there. Four-man job. So make sure you're waitin' for us on the corner at midnight. Cos if you're nor there, know wor we're gonna do?'

'Wor?'

'Come and ger you!'

They meant it. Iggy shuddered. He was cornered.

'Thar clear?' whispered Mark.

'Yeah.'

'So wor you gonna do, Ig?'

'Be there.'

'Thass a good boy. I knew you'd come round in the end.'

Mark patted him softly on the cheek then walked away. Pug and Elroy went after him. They had beaten Iggy into submission. He had nobody to turn to for support. He was not really a member of their gang. They were just using him.

Iggy was doomed.

Saturday night found June Higgins sitting in front of the mirror on her dressing table and putting the final touches to her make-up. She had had her hair cut in a new style and she had bought some new perfume. The odour pervaded the bedroom.

Now that the children knew about Rob Ford, she wanted to sell him to them as much as she could. He had been kind to her and she tried to tell them why. But they were remote and detached. They eyed Rob with intense suspicion.

It was going to take time. A lot of time.

Gail came into the room and stood beside her.

'Wass thar smell?'

'My perfume. Stephanotis.'

'Where you goin', Mum?'

'The usual. For a drink or two.'

'With 'im?'

'Yeah.' She turned to her daughter. 'Rob is a nice man wenn you ger to know him. Try, Gail. For my sake. Will you?'

Eyes laden with resentment, the girl pulled away.

'Rob is my friend,' said June. 'And yours.'

The doorbell rang and Gail was startled.

'That'll be Rob now. Why don't you go and ler 'im in?'

But the girl shrank back once again.

June went through to the door and opened it. Rob appraised her with a grin and nodded his approval. He was wearing a blue suit that was a bit too tight for him. His hair was plastered down with Brylcreem.

'I'll just be a tick, love,' said June. 'Almost ready.'

'OK.'

'Did you buy wor I suggested?' she whispered.

'Eh? Oh, yeah.'

Rob Ford walked into the living room and thrust his hand into his pocket. As Gail looked up at him, he pulled out a packet of Smarties and offered it to her.

'D'you like these?'

She nodded and took them but her expression did not alter.

'Where's Ian?' he asked.

'In his bedroom.'

'Ian!' shouted June. 'Come out of there!'

'Always 'ides away when I come,' noted Rob with a scowl. 'Wass wrong with me, June? BO or somethin'?'

Iggy's head popped out from his bedroom.

'Hello, Ian,' said Rob, manufacturing another smile.

'Oh . . . hello.'

'Bought you these.'

Iggy took his packet of Smarties but he could not even pretend to be grateful. June shot him a reproachful look but it had no effect on him.

'We'll be back late,' she said.

'Very late,' added Rob.

'You're to be in bed by nine, Gail.'

'Aw, Mum!'

'Ten-thirty for you, Ian. OK?'

'Yeah,' he murmured.

'Sleep tight!'

June did not bother with a token kiss for them. She was eager to be away. Calling a farewell, she went out with Rob and climbed down the steps towards the waiting transit van.

Iggy glanced down at the Smarties in his hand. He held them out to his sister and she ran across to snatch them.

'Doan you wann them?' she asked.

'Nor from 'im.'

Iggy went back into his room and lay on the bed. It was not long past seven o'clock. In five hours' time, he had to meet the others at Woodfield school.

Then his life would never be the same again.

Chapter Ten

The club was absolutely packed. It was a cauldron of throbbing sound and pulsing light. Couples were dancing everywhere as the disco beat drove on and on. A pall of cigarette smoke hung over the place. The temperature seemed to go up by the minute.

Mark Stavros, Pug Anderson and Elroy Cooper had been there for a couple of hours. They were not old enough to join the club but they had got in nevertheless. Mark had brought Lynne while Elroy was with Ruth. Once again Pug spent his time at the bar. There was no partner for him.

The friends reeled off the dance floor in the middle of a record. Lynne and Ruth were peeved.

'Why carn we dance on?' complained Lynne.

'I was juss gerrin' goin',' said Ruth.

'We 'ave to love you and leave you,' explained Mark.

'*Now*?'

'Gone eleven, Ruthie,' said Elroy. 'We gor work to do.'

'Where?' asked Lynne.

'Never you mind,' said Mark. 'Juss stay right 'ere.'

'We'll be back!' promised Elroy.

'Why carn we come with you?' asked Ruth.

'Because you're our alibi,' Mark told them. 'You can say thar we were 'ere all the time.' He gave Lynne a kiss. 'Thass to keep you goin' while I'm gone.'

'Doan be too long,' she purred.

'We won't be,' said Elroy. 'Enjoy yourselves, girls.'

'Ready?' called Pug, elbowing his way towards them.

'Yeah,' replied Mark. 'Come on, El.'

They left the two girls dancing with each other and made their way to the exit. When they came out into the dark, the cold night air hit them like a punch.

'Wor now?' grunted Pug.

'Collect our gear and ger started,' said Mark.

'I feel great,' announced Elroy, still moving to the beat of the music. 'I'm gonna dance right through thar old school!'

They set off up the precinct in a tight bunch.

'Wor abour Iggy?' wondered Pug.

'Fogerrim,' advised Mark.

'Suppose he doan turn up?'

'Oh, Ig'll be there!' guaranteed Elroy.

'Berra be!' growled Pug.

'Doan worry, mate,' soothed Mark. 'Me and Elroy left nothin' to chance, 'ave we, El? It'll all go like clockwork. Iggy wudden dare to ler us down now.'

They hurried on towards their rendezvous.

Iggy was tormented by all the things that could hold him up. Suppose his mother came back just as he was leaving? Suppose Gail woke up? Suppose some of the neighbours saw him going?

Suppose the police spotted him?

Time dragged by with excruciating slowness as he waited for the moment to slip away. Gail went to bed at the prescribed time but she read some books for a long time. When he tiptoed in to her, she had fallen asleep and left her light on. Iggy switched it off then listened to the regular sound of her breathing.

He was reassured. Gail would not wake up now.

Iggy went back to his own room and took a final look at himself in the mirror. They had told him to wear dark clothes. He had his black jeans on, his navy sweater and his black trainers. His anorak was a dark green and his woolly hat was brown.

He checked his watch for the umpteenth time then he braced himself for the adventure. It was time to go.

Switching off the light, he closed his bedroom door after him as soundlessly as he could. He was trembling with nerves already but there was no help for it. He simply had to go.

Iggy opened the front door and stepped out.

This was it.

A few cars and the occasional taxi went by, raking the road ahead with their full beams. Otherwise it was a quiet night. Nobody noticed the tubby figure who loped along the pavement in the shadows. He was well-camouflaged.

When he got to the rendezvous, Iggy had his first shock. They were not there. Mark had been so specific about the time that he could not believe it. Where were they? Had they got him here as some kind of practical joke? Was it all a hoax?

He stepped out into the open and peered around. Three figures suddenly jumped on him without warning.

'Gerrim!'

''old 'im tight!'

'Grab 'is wallet!'

'Search 'is pockets!'

Iggy thought he was being mugged then he recognized the laughter. It was them. Having a bit of fun at his expense.

'Scare you?' said Elroy.

'Yeah!'

'Iss OK,' consoled Mark. 'We're on your side really.'

'Anyway,' remarked Pug, 'you gor nothin' worth pinchin'.'

Mark called them to order and gave them their instructions. They made their way in single file to the dining hall and shinned up the drainpipe one at a time. Iggy was the last to climb it and he had a lot of difficulty.

With the aid of Mark's cupped hands, Elroy again got up on to the roof of the main building. He threw down a rope to haul the others up. Two of them were needed to yank Iggy aloft.

Cool as a cucumber, Mark gave all the orders.

'Elroy.'

'Yeah.'

'Tie the other rope to thar water tank. Juss in case we need a rear exit.'

'OK, boss,' hissed Elroy and ran off.

'Pug.'

'Wor?'

'Keep a lookout over the front of the school.'

'Leave it to me.'

While Pug moved off, Mark and Iggy went over to one of the circular windows in the roof of the science block. Even in the gloom, they looked as if they might be a formidable obstacle. But Mark was equal to the task.

'Shine the torch 'ere, Ig,' he said.

'Right.'

'Keep the beam down!' he hissed.

'Sorry.'

'We're norra flippin' lighthouse!'

Iggy aimed the beam at the first of the clamps. The bolts were thick and filmed with rust but Mark had the right tools for the job. They creaked when he twisted them then gave more freely. One by one, he was able to remove the clamps altogether.

'Now for the bess bit!' he whispered.

'Wass thar?'

'Watch!'

Grabbing hold of the circular, convex window, Mark

rolled it a yard or so to the right. Iggy felt an excitement. As he shone the torch into the aperture, he could see right down into the corridor beside the science lab.

They were in Lambo's domain.

Elroy now arrived with the other rope. Tying one end around a knob on the parapet he dropped the other down through the hole.

'There you are!'

'Perfect, El.'

'Who's goin' in?' asked Iggy.

'All of us!'

Mark signalled to Pug who crept over to them at speed.

'Nuthin' over there,' he reported.

'What are we waitin' for?' said Mark.

He slid down the rope and landed in the corridor. Elroy followed, then Pug and then Iggy. The feeling of exhilaration was spreading now. They were all on air.

Elroy did a little jig up and down the corridor. Pug took an aerosol spray from his pocket and started to adorn the cream walls with graffiti. Mark nudged Iggy.

'Glad you came now?'

'Yeah.'

'Less take a look around!'

The four of them trotted along the corridor until they came to the staircase. They went down to the ground floor in single file. Pug was still busy with his spray. Every wall he passed got the treatment.

They stopped outside a door off the entrance hall.

'This the storeroom?' said Iggy.

'Yeah,' explained Mark. 'Gor the lot. Radios, tellies, cassette recorders, photographic equipment.'

'You name it, we nick it!' said Pug with a chuckle.

'Bur iss locked,' noted Iggy.

'Nor for long, said Mark. 'El – do your stuff.'

Elroy took out a large bunch of keys and started trying

them in the lock. It only took him a few minutes to find one that fitted. He lifted the handle as he twisted the key.

The door swung back on its hinges.

'Open sesame!'

Iggy shone the torch into the storeroom. It was piled high with expensive equipment of all sorts. Mark and Elroy dived in to sort out the most portable items. Pug examined it all with approval.

'Good stuff, this. We should make a fortune.'

He stepped into the storeroom to help the others.

'Any video cassettes here?'

'Dozens,' said Elroy.

'Gimme a few.'

As Iggy held the torch for them, his attitude slowly began to change. There had been a thrill at the moment of entry but it soon faded. What replaced it was a kind of disgust. The other three were nothing but common thieves. They were there to pillage the school. Iggy took no pleasure from that. He wanted no part of the stealing.

His three colleagues invited him in.

'Come and join us, Ig.'

'Grab worrever you like, mate.'

'Feel free.'

But Iggy was now feeling deep revulsion. He could not bear to touch any of the stolen goods. It all belonged to Woodfield. His instinct was to put it all back.

The others were caught up in what they were doing. Their voices became progressively more excited.

'Your turn next, Ig.'

'Soon as we finish 'ere.'

'We'll lug this stuff back upstairs then you can 'ave your fun. Elroy will open the lab for you.'

'Lambo's private retreat!'

'All yours to destroy in any way you like.'

'You can 'it the place like an atom bomb!'

'Juss wait till Lambo sees it on Monday!'

Iggy did not join in the laughter. Nor did he relish the idea of running amok in the science laboratory. The notion of getting his own back on Lambo appealed to him at first. After all, she had done a lot to hurt him. Lambo had humiliated him in front of the class. Got him sent to the Sin Bin. Made him pump up her tyres again. Iggy loathed her. But that did not mean he wanted to take her laboratory apart. That was senseless.

Mark, Pug and Elroy came out of the storeroom.

'Like Aladdin's Cave in here,' said Mark.

'Riches all round you, like!' agreed Pug.

'All thanks to my magic keys,' boasted Elroy.

They began to gather up their spoils.

'Gimme an 'and, Iggy,' said Mark.

But the boy held back. He was quietly appalled.

'Wass up?' asked Mark.

'Nothin'.'

'Then shift some of this for us.'

Iggy shrugged. He was rooted to the spot.

'Doan conk out on us now!' moaned Elroy.

'Wassa marra?' teased Pug. 'Afraid to ger 'is 'ands dirty?'

'We need your help!' urged Mark.

'So ger busy!' ordered Pug.

'We're all in this together,' Elroy reminded him.

Iggy did not know what to do. He was involved in the robbery. There was no getting away from that. It was no use having scruples now. On the other hand, he just could not bring himself to handle the stolen goods.

'Wake up, Iggy!' called Mark. 'Do something.'

The decision was immediately taken out of the younger boy's hands. Out of the corner of his eye, he saw a large torch beam approaching the main entrance. The others saw it, too.

'Jesus H. Christ!'

'Iss Charlie!'

'Less gerrout of 'ere!'

'Wor about all this?'

'Leave it – juss run!'

The three of them took to their heels and tore along the corridor towards the stairs. Iggy came to life when he heard the Alsatian barking. It sounded mean and hungry.

As he sprinted after the others, he heard the caretaker inserting a key into the front door. The next second, the alarm was set off and the whole school vibrated with noise. It was quite deafening.

'Wait for me!' howled Iggy.

'Come on, then!' encouraged Mark. 'You can do it!'

'Help!'

Iggy went up the stairs and into the corridor in the science block. The rope dangled invitingly down. Mark and Elroy had already pulled themselves up it and Pug was now doing so. His legs disappeared through the opening as Iggy arrived.

Mark dragged him up then he peered down through the hole.

'Climb up, Ig!'

'I can't!'

'You gorra. Less you wanna be cort.'

The barking of the Alsatian was coming closer all the time. It added a new dimension of horror. Iggy threw himself at the rope and tried to climb up but his weight was against him. Mark stayed long enough to make a grab for him. To no avail. Iggy was out of reach. Mark decided to save his own skin.

'Doan give us away, Ig!' he hissed.

'Help me up!'

'Say nothin'! Gorrit?'

'I wann to come out!'

But it was not to be.

107

While the others made good their escape down the rope from the water tank, Iggy dangled helplessly in the corridor. The dog came bounding towards him and judged its leap.

'Aghhhhh!'

Iggy yelled as the animal sank its teeth into his anorak and pulled him to the floor in a heap. Before the dog could attack him, its master curbed it with a command.

'Stay!'

It went down on all fours right opposite Iggy, watching his every move. Charlie came charging up with a torch in his hand. He shone it in Iggy's face.

'Nor you again!'

'Sorry . . .'

The events of that night were so confused and frantic that they became a blur in Iggy's mind. He was taken off by the police and questioned at length about what had happened. His mother was dragged down to the police station in the small hours. A solicitor was hastily rustled up. There was a brief appearance in court. Iggy was granted bail. They let him go free but only for a matter of time. The court case still hung over him.

'Who *were* they?' demanded Froggie.

'Wor, sir?'

'The others. Give us their names.'

'There were no others.'

'Don't lie to me, boy,. You must've had help.'

'No, sir. On my own.'

'You're shielding criminals.'

'There was only me.'

'Thieves and vandals!' wailed Froggie. 'They tried to strip Woodfield of some of its finest equipment. I want to track them down. I want every last name.'

'I was by myself, sir.'

The headmaster gave up. He had harangued the boy for half an hour without success. The police would have to find the others who were involved. Iggy was far too young and inexperienced to plan a raid on that scale. He was one of a team.

'You've let Woodfield down, Higgins.'

'Didden mean to, sir.'

'The publicity will ruin us.'

They were in Froggie's study and the boy was sitting in a chair in the middle of the room. Froggie was circling him like a light aircraft waiting to come in to land. Confident that he could break the boy down, he got nowhere with him. Iggy had clammed up and would admit nothing.

'I hope you're proud of yourself, Higgins.'

'No, sir.'

'You helped to cause hundreds of pounds' worth of damage.'

'I know.'

'So who were your accomplices?'

'Nobody.'

'Tell the truth!' howled Froggie. 'It will be best for you in the long run. Who organized it?'

'I did, sir.'

'Nonsense! How many others were there?'

'Dunno.'

'Are they boys from the school?'

'Dunno.'

'How were you recruited?'

'Dunno, sir.'

Eventually, Froggie gave up. He could get nothing out of the boy. Meanwhile, he had to take him back into the school until his court case came up.

'Wor 'appens to me now, sir?' said Iggy.

'You go back to the Sin Bin!'

'Oh!'

'In solitary confinement, if need be!'

Iggy was unperturbed. When you have been attacked by an Alsatian while dangling helplessly from a rope, you are not afraid of an interview with your headmaster. The worst, Iggy felt, was over. There was nothing they could do to upset him. It was a very calming thought.

Froggie Parsons savoured his sense of outrage.

'I've never seen such blatant disregard for property.'

'Sorry, sir.'

'And to think that Mrs Lambert wanted me to bring you out of the Annexe! What a mistake that would have been.'

'Mrs Lambert?'

'You managed to take her in. But not me, sir.'

Iggy let it all wash over him. His mind was on something far more important. His arrest had yielded an incidental bonus. It had been necessary to inform both his parents. The police had tracked down Vance Higgins in no time. He lived in Acock's Green in Birmingham. Iggy now had his father's address.

It was a start.

Chapter Eleven

Basher Bowen took it personally. He saw it as a reflection on him. The Sin Bin was supposed to bank down any unruly elements in the school. It had now done the opposite. Ian Higgins of 4C was a docile and obedient boy when he went to the Annexe. In a short space of time, he was transformed into a vandal who attacked a teacher's car and a thief who broke into the school itself.

Don Sheen tried to talk it through with his colleague. He astounded Basher by suggesting that Mrs Lambert should be involved in the discussion. But Lambo duly came.

The three of them sat in the upstairs staff room at the Annexe. Tea had been made to Lambo's specifications. It put her in a mood to lead off.

'I warned the headmaster,' she said. 'Put a boy like Higgins with some real delinquents and something is bound to rub off on him.'

'I couldn't agree more, Mrs Lambert,' said Don.

'It's not as simple as that,' argued Basher. 'We've had all sorts in here. Sometimes it's the hard cases who crumble. They get softened up by being with the more civilized kids. See what I mean? It can work both ways.'

'Not with Ian Higgins,' asserted Lambo.

'No,' supported Don. 'He came here and went straight into a downward spiral.'

'How do we get him out of it?' asked Basher.

'Plenty of care and understanding,' urged Lambo.

'That's Don's prescription, too,' observed Basher. 'Left to him, every kid in the school would have his own personal shrink. He'd turn the whole place into a nuthouse.'

'It already *is* a nuthouse,' quipped Don. 'All I want to do is to humanize the staff and rescue the pupils.'

'From what?'

'The pressures.'

'Dieu! That word again!'

'OK, it's a cliché,' agreed Don, 'but it still contains a lot of truth. Ian Higgins cracked up because the pressures on the kid were just too big.'

'How do we relieve those pressures?' asked Lambo.

'Go easy on him here, for a start.'

'Not on your life, Don!'

'He needs guidance, Bryn!'

'Aye, mun. The guidance of strong discipline. Just let me get my hands on him again. I'll knock some sense into him.'

'Bullying is no education!' said Don.

'Oh, I'm in favour of a certain amount of discipline,' admitted Lambo. 'You've got to subdue the kids before you can teach them anything. On the other hand, a more liberal approach sometimes works.'

'Not in the Sin Bin!' insisted Basher.

'You're behind the times, Bryn.'

'I've learned to live with my disability.'

'Don't be sarcastic.'

'Coming back to Ian Higgins,' said Lambo. 'I think we should ask him.'

'Ask him what?' wondered Basher.

'How we can best help him.'

'The boy is disturbed,' reasoned Don. 'He doesn't know what kind of help he needs. That's the trouble.'

'It's the teacher's job to teach,' insisted Basher. 'We can't have pupils telling us what *they'd* like.'

'Why not?' said Don.

'It's like asking the tail to wag the dog.'

Lambo checked her watch then finished her tea.

'I have to get back to the main school, I'm afraid,' she apologized, 'but I leave you with one thought. Don here likes a gentle, understanding approach. Bryn prefers iron discipline. I'm somewhere between the two. That gives Ian a pretty wide choice. *One* of us must be suitable, surely?'

'Yes,' agreed Don. 'All we have to do is find out which of those three it is.'

Being a school celebrity had a tawdry glamour for the first few days. Iggy was treated with everything from respect to hero-worship. Kids flocked around him whenever he arrived at school. Questions assailed him on all sides.

When the pleasure wore off, it became rather tedious. He had no privacy, no rest. Besides, his notoriety was based upon his arrest. His trial was yet to come. When he thought about what might actually happen to him in court, Iggy was sobered. There was no glamour in a custodial sentence. He longed for the old days. Ian Higgins of 4C. Gentle anonymity.

Fortunately, he still had Samantha Jarrett as a friend. A walk to school with her was always a tonic.

'Wor 'ave you done abour your father?' she asked.

'Nuthin' yet.'

'Why nor?'

'Because I'm not sure 'ow to go abour it.'

'Thort of writing?'

'Can't seem to find the right words.'

'I'll help you,' she said. 'If you'd let me.'

'Oh yes! Thanks.'

'Will you tell your mum?'

'No!'

'Why nor?'

'She duzzen care abour Dad – or me.'

113

'You think it's all her fault, then?'

'Doan you?'

'Nor really.'

'Sam, she drove Dad out.'

'Is that what she told you?'

'Well, no . . .'

'Then where did you ger the idea?'

'It's obvious.'

'Not to me.'

They crossed a road and struck off towards Woodfield.
Iggy was annoyed that she was defending his mother. It
was much more convenient for him to have someone whom
he could blame for just about everything. His mother fitted
that bill.

'You ever talk to 'er?' wondered Sam.

'Course. All the time.'

'Real talk, I mean. Like this.'

'Mum duzzen go in for thar, really.'

'Maybe you doan give 'er the chance.' Sam gave a shrug.
'If she was my mum, there's a lorra talkin' I'd wanna do
with 'er. I know that. First thing I'd ask 'er is about the
boyfriend.'

'Can't bear 'im.'

'*She* can, Ian. Wudden you like to know why?'

'Dunno.'

'It might explain a lorra things.'

'Eh?'

'Like why she didden ger on with your dad.'

'Bur she did!' he said with vehemence. 'Thort he was
great. They was very 'appy. I know thar for a fact.'

'Do you?'

Iggy considered it. Suddenly, he was less certain. Perhaps
there had been a rift between his parents. The one thing
that he felt sure about was that his mother engineered the
break-up.

114

'Talk to 'er,' urged Sam once again.

'Wor about?'

'Everythin'.'

'Bur she never lissens, Sam.'

'You're the one who oughta do the lissenin'.'

They walked on in silence for a while. He had plenty to turn over in his mind. Something made its way to the surface.

'Sam.'

'Yeah?'

'Can I arsk you a favour?'

'As long as iss nor abour Pug Anderson!'

'Nothin' like thar.'

'Good.'

'If . . . anythin' 'appens to me . . .'

'At the trial, you mean?'

'Yeah. If they do lock me up . . .'

'Go on. Arsk.'

'Would-you-write-to-me-like?' he gabbled.

'Try stoppin' me!'

'Thass fantastic! Thanks.'

His load had lightened all of a sudden. With Sam in his corner, he felt that he could cope with the trial. She would help him through it.

June Higgins had been rocked by the news of her son's arrest. She was flabbergasted to learn that he had actually left his sister all alone in the flat when he sneaked off to take part in a raid on his school. It made her feel that she just did not know her own son. They were growing apart.

Rob Ford was less than sympathetic about it all.

'Doan keep goin' on abour 'im,' he complained.

'Bur 'e's my son!'

'Kids are bound to ger into trouble now and again,' he said dismissively. 'I know I did. Only natural.'

'Ian was always such a quiet boy in the past.'

'They're the worst.'

'I wish *you'd* 'ave a chat with 'im, Rob.'

'Me?'

'Yeah. Sort of man to man.'

'Bur 'e's nor *my* son, June.'

'Makes no difference . . . Would you?'

'I'll see,' he said with obvious distaste.

They were sitting in the corner of the pub that had now become their regular haunt. Rob drained his glass of beer and stood up to go to the bar for a refill. When he reached for her empty glass as well, she put her hand over it.

'Wassa marrer with you?' he demanded.

'I wanna go back 'ome, Rob.'

'Bur you come out for a night with me!'

He moved her hand, took the glass then went across to the bar. Ordering another beer and a dry martini, he paid for them and picked them up. When he turned around, however, he had a surprise.

June Higgins was not there. She had walked out.

Mark Stavros was serving behind the counter at the fish and chip shop. Elroy Cooper was waiting for him to finish so that they could go out together. Both youths had the cocky, over-confident look of someone who has got away with something. Iggy was taking the rap for them. They were in the clear.

Mark served a customer then turned to chat to Elroy.

'Where's Pug?'

'Dunno. Expected 'im ages ago.'

'Yeah. Usually lost a coupla quid on the fruit machine by now.' Mark grinned. 'Never learns, does 'e?'

The shop was empty now. Elroy made sure that they could not be overheard then he leaned across the counter towards his friend. His voice was a hoarse whisper.

'You think we can really trust 'im?'

'Who?'

'Iggy. If he sings, we'd be in the cack.'

'Not an earthly!' assured Mark. 'I put the 'fluence on Ig. Terrified to admit he even knows me ler alone anythin' else.'

'We're 'ome and dry then.'

'More or less.'

'Supposin' 'e breaks down in court?'

'Take ir easy, El. Doan ger so uptight. Iggy's OK.'

'Hope so.'

Tony Stavros came out to put some fresh chips in the vat. The conversation changed at once. The older man talked nostalgically about the warm climate of his home-land. He would much rather be in Cyprus than in Britain at that time of the year.

Two men in raincoats came into the shop and approached the counter. Mark gave them a welcoming smile and made ready to serve them.

'What can I get you, gentlemen?' he said.

'Are you Mark Stavros?' asked one of them.

'Yeah. Why?'

The man took out his wallet and showed his warrant card.

'Police.'

Mark, Tony and Elroy reacted with alarm.

The detective stated his business.

'We'd like to interview you in connection with a robbery last Saturday night at Woodfield Comprehensive School.'

'Bur I 'ad nothin' to do with it!' protested Mark.

'Where were you around midnight that day?' asked the detective quietly.

'At a disco with my mates. Elroy here and Pug Anderson.'

'Yes,' returned the detective. 'Mr Anderson is already

helping us with our inquiries.' He confronted Elroy. 'And we'll be needing a chat with you as well, sir.'

'Oh,' murmured Elroy.

Tony Stavros was now twitching with anxiety.

'You in trouble again, Mark?'

'No, Dad. Iss all a mistake.'

'Did you really go to that disco,' said his father.

'Yes! We took Lynne and Ruth. We gor dozens of witnesses.'

Tony looked to the first detective for an explanation.

'What is this all about, officer?'

The detective gave an enigmatic smile.

'Fingerprints.'

Gail Higgins had taken it worst of all. The news that her brother was involved in a crime had hit her hard. She was still dazed. Iggy played cards with her on the kitchen table. They were both surprised to hear raised voices coming up the stairs outside. Their mother was not expected back for some hours.

A key was put in the lock and the door opened.

June stepped in and turned to dismiss Rob Ford.

'I carn ask you in . . . Goodnight.'

'Wor is this?' said Rob angrily.

'We'll talk abour it another time.'

'No, we won't,' he insisted. 'We'll talk about it now.'

He forced the door open and came into the living room.

'Would you please get out of my flat?' she ordered.

'Nobody gives me the brush-off!' he warned.

'Rob, lissen – '

'And doan you try to soft-soap me either. Cos it woan work. Wass gor into you all of a sudden?'

'You must be blind nor to notice.'

'Ian and the cops?'

118

'I'm worried sick abour it,' she exploded. 'And all you can talk abour is cars and holidays and real ale.'

Rob was about to answer her when he saw the two faces in the doorway of the kitchen. Iggy and Gail were watching him with a mixture of dislike and apprehension.

'Disappear, you two!'

'This is their home!' June reminded him hotly. 'Doan you push my children around, Rob Ford.'

'Then doan you try it on with me.'

'I wanned to come back, thass all.'

'Cos I was borin' you, I suppose.'

'No – because my children need me.'

'Bit late to think abour thar, innit?' he sneered. 'You never bothered abour it before. Wor were you doin' Saturday night while Ian was breaking into his school? Carin' for your kids?'

'Gerrout!' she snapped.

'I'll stay as long as I like.'

'Wann me to go to the police?'

It was a frightening moment. They confronted each other in the middle of the room like two animals raring for a fight. Iggy had seen enough. He took Gail back into the kitchen and shut the door. The girl was trembling.

The row started up again and abuse was hurled to and fro. Iggy did not listen to the words. He sat there and suffered, blaming his mother for bringing such a violent and foul-mouthed man into the flat. Rob's voice rose to a screech then they heard the front door open and slam. He was gone.

Gail broke away from Iggy to run out to her mother. June comforted her and assured her that Rob would never be coming again. As they cuddled on the sofa, they did not see Iggy letting himself out. He had had enough of his mother and her tantrums. He would go where he was really wanted.

* * *

119

It was well over twenty miles to Birmingham and the weather was icy. Iggy cycled along as fast as he could but it still took an age. It was quite late when he finally arrived in Acock's Green. His exhaustion was tempered by the realization that he had made the break with his mother. June had rejected him all these years. Now he was rejecting her.

He asked for the street he wanted and was disappointed to find the houses rather small and the area run-down. A few stray dogs roamed about. The weather gave it all a rather bleak aspect.

When he tracked down the number he was after, he rang the bell. There was a long wait then he heard heavy footsteps descending the stairs. The door opened.

A big, strapping man in a working shirt and jeans stood there. He blinked at Iggy uncomprehendingly then slowly he recognized him. The man ran a hand through his shock of red hair.

Iggy felt a surge of pride go through him.

'Hello, Dad,' he said.

Chapter Twelve

Vance Higgins was torn between surprise and embarrassment. He needed a few moments to take it all in. He had put on weight since he had left home. There was a slightly vanquished air to him. He glanced around uneasily.

'Wor are you doin' 'ere?' he asked.

'I come to see you.'

'Does your mum know?'

'No,' replied Iggy, shaking his head. 'I sneaked out.'

'Why?'

'Cos I'd rather be 'ere, Dad.'

Vance studied him balefully then gave a nervous smile.

'You berra come in.'

'Thanks, Dad.'

'You cycle all the way?'

'Yeah. Took me 'ours.'

'Leave the bike there.'

Iggy parked the machine against the wall and followed his father into the house. It was small and badly-lit but it seemed to be comfortable enough.

'This all yours, Dad?' asked the boy, desperate to be impressed.

'Er, no . . . Juss the flat upstairs.'

Vance Higgins trotted up the carpeted stairs to the front bedroom. It was furnished as a bedsitter with a sofa, a double bed, a table, some upright chairs, a chest of drawers, a wardrobe and an electric stove all jumbled in together.

Iggy noticed only one thing.

There was a woman sprawled on the sofa.

She was dark-haired and buxom with round, flashing

121

eyes set in a pallid face. The woman wore a quilted housecoat and a pair of pink fur-edged slippers. She was about the same age as Vance but looked much older without any make-up on.

Seeing that they had a visitor, she pulled her housecoat around her and put a hand to her hair.

'Who's this, then?' she said.

'Ian,' muttered Vance.

'Who?'

'My son.'

'Oh!'

She got to her feet in alarm and looked down at him. Her lips drew back in a half-smile then she shot Vance a reproving look. Iggy felt even more uneasy.

'Er . . . this is Brenda,' introduced Vance awkwardly.

'Hello, Ian,' she said.

'Hello.'

'Rather late for a social call,' she observed in her sing-song Birmingham accent. 'We wern expectin' visitors, like.'

'Ian cycled all the way.'

'Wor for?'

'To see Dad,' murmured the boy.

In those first few minutes in the room, Iggy understood things about his parents that he had never realized before. Vance had not been driven out by his wife at all. He had left her for this other woman, this rather fleshy and dramatic creature in the housecoat.

An accusatory note came into her voice.

'You been in trouble with the police, 'avven you?'

'Sort of.'

'They came and told Vance.'

'Thass right,' agreed his father. 'Um . . . sit down, Ian.'

'Ta.'

Brenda scooped up some magazines from the sofa to make room for him. Then she plonked herself beside him.

122

Vance perched on an upright chair and ran a hand through his hair again.

'Looks like you, Vance,' decided Brenda.

'Think so?

'Same eyes, like. Same nose.'

'Carn see it myself.'

'Men never can,' she scolded.

Iggy was completely out of his depth. He had persuaded himself that his father would be in much bigger and better accommodation, and that he would be so pleased to see his son that he would snatch him up in his arms. The idea that Vance might be living with someone did not even cross his mind. Now he was faced with the reality, he was stunned.

'Gail OK?' mumbled his father.

'Yeah.'

'Still at Cameron Road?'

'Yeah.'

Iggy made an effort to salvage something from the visit.

'Villa're doin' well.'

'Ah.'

'See a lorra matches, Dad?'

'Nor really, son.'

'Villa Park's nor far away, though.'

'I carn *stand* football,' interrupted Brenda. 'Vance tried to take me once bur I was bored rigid, like. Doan see wor all the fuss is abour myself.'

Iggy's last illusion was shattered. He had carefully preserved the image of a man who was so dedicated to his team that he would follow them through thick and thin. Instead of that, Vance Higgins had more or less abandoned the game. He had other priorities now.

The boy jumped involuntarily to his feet.

'Berra be goin'!'

'Already?' said Vance.

'We doan wanna 'old Ian up,' added Brenda, rising to her feet. 'Snorra as if he can stay 'ere. No room for 'im.'

'Where will you go, son?'

'I'll be OK.'

'Sure?'

'Yeah, Dad.'

Iggy shuffled his way across to the door. He nodded a goodbye to Brenda then dived out. Vance followed him down the stairs, worried about the boy yet relieved that he was going. Two separate worlds had connected in the bedsitter and it had been a harrowing experience. He wanted to leave his wife and children in the past. They belonged to another Vance Higgins.

'Er, sorry abour this, Ian.'

'Thass OK.'

'Tell your mum . . . tell 'er I been a bit stretched for cash lately. Thas why I didden send any, like. Bur I will. Wenn I ger sorted out.'

'Bye, Dad.'

'Go easy with thar bike now.'

'Yeah.'

He opened the door and Iggy went out into the night.

The darkness hid the tears in the boy's eyes.

June Higgins spent a sleepless night of tearful anxiety at Clearview. When Iggy did not return by midnight, she contacted the police. They searched in the locality but there was no sign of him. They got in touch with Birmingham police who, in turn, paid another visit to Vance. He told them what time the boy had left. The search broadened. Iggy could be anywhere.

Early next morning, Samantha Jarrett came calling.

'Hello, Mrs 'iggins.'

'Hello.'

'Any news?'

'No.'

'Like me to take Gail to school for you?'

'I'm keepin' 'er 'ome today.'

'Anythin' else I can do?'

'No, thanks. Bur iss kind of you to come up.'

'Ian'll be back,' insisted the girl. 'I know 'im.'

'The worry's been drivin' me mad.'

Sam nodded and squeezed her arm. Then she went back down the stairs to her own flat. She had to give Kevin his breakfast and take him off to school. Everybody in Clearview had heard about Iggy by now. There would be plenty of support for June from her friends and neighbours.

Sam tried to battle with her own fears. Iggy had been out alone in a long, cold, hostile night. She prayed that no harm had come to him.

Where on earth could he be?

Routine dominated Mrs Lambert's life at home as well as at work. Because she had a disabled husband, she had to be up very early to see to him. When they had had breakfast, she drove off to school so that she could get there before most people arrived. There was something about being the first in the car park that appealed to her and she often managed it.

That morning, however, someone had got to school before her.

She did not spot him at first. It was only when she was getting out of her car that her attention was caught. A large bundle was wrapped up in the corner of the empty bike sheds. When she took a closer look, she saw that it was a boy, lying on the concrete floor in a cycling cape.

It was Iggy.

She bent down to see to him at once.

As soon as she touched his shoulder, he roused.

'Are you all right, Ian?' she asked with concern.

125

'Mmm.'

'What are you doing out here?'

'Went . . . to sleep . . .'

'Gracious! You've been here all *night*!'

He was wearing an anorak under his cape and that had kept out most of the cold, but he was obviously chilled and weak. Mrs Lambert summoned the caretaker and they carried the boy into the school. They put him on the bed in the warm medical room. A hot cup of tea restored him and he was able to sit up. He was still not sure how he finished up in the bike sheds. It was all rather hazy.

Charlie rang the police to tell them that the boy had been found. Word was immediately sent by patrol car to Clearview. As soon as the school nurse arrived, she examined the boy but found no serious injury or damage.

Iggy was simply exhausted. What he needed was a long sleep in his own bed. The police arrived to take him home but Mrs Lambert insisted that she went with them. Iggy raised no objection. He dozed off in the back of the car.

June Higgins was waiting anxiously for him to arrive. She threw herself on him when he was lifted out of the car and wept copiously all the way up the stairs. Mrs Lambert went into the flat with her. The police tactfully withdrew.

Iggy was put to bed and the women sat either side of him.

It was strange. He was being looked after by the two women he thought he hated. Yet those feelings had gone now.

He was actually glad to be home.

The season of goodwill finally penetrated the Sin Bin. Under the supervision of Basher Bowen, they put up decorations and made the old house into a warm and welcoming place once more. On the last day of term, they even had a Christmas party. There was food, drink,